Rescue Me

A Study Guide

Sylvia D. Carter

Sylvia Carter Ministries

COLLEGE PARK, GEORGIA

Sylvia D. Carter/Sylvia Carter Ministries
3695 Roosevelt Highway
College Park/Georgia/USA 30349
www.sylviacarterunlocked.com

Book Layout © 2017 BookDesignTemplates.com
Cover Design: Galen Ross
Editing: Edith W. Anderson
Publisher Sylvia Carter Ministries
Rescue Me/ Sylvia D. Carter. -- 1st ed.
ISBN 978-1-7336230-2-5

Dedication

This book is for every person restlessly searching for their place of fulfillment in God. Each of us has a unique calling—when we allow God to put His super on our natural, He can do extraordinary things through us. We are each uniquely and creatively made with specific skills, passions, and talents. Remember your purpose was assigned and when you have the understanding of who God created you to be, then your purpose will be discovered. Jeremiah 29:11 says, *"For I know the plans I have for you," declares the LORD, plans to prosper you and not to harm you, plans to give you hope and a future."*

In Psalm 139:13-16, the psalmist declares, "Because I am fearfully and wonderfully made; your works are wonderful, I know that full well. My frame was not hidden from you when I was made in the secret place, when I was woven together in the depths of the earth. Your eyes saw my unformed body; all the days ordained for me were written in your book before one of them came to be."

I am expecting the Lord to rescue me again, so that once again I will see his goodness to me here in the land of the living.

PSALM 27:13 TLB

ACKNOWLEDGEMENTS

Thank you, Father God, for all you have done for me; your love overwhelms me and I shall forever love and praise your name. To everyone who has been persistent in asking me when? It was the constant support and encouragement of each of you that have allowed this work to come to fruition. To my extended family and my parents, I love you dearly. Sandra, you are a sweetheart—thank you! To Siloam Church International, it's a forever and a day thing with us! To all of you who have been kind enough to read anything I have written, my heart is filled with appreciation. To my Sylvia Carter Unlocked team thank you for pushing me—hard! To my husband and my children, love and hugs.

TABLE OF CONTENTS

Rescued by Bitter Water...1

Rescued by the Power of Prayer 11

Rescued During the Darkness of Depression 23

Rescued from Unhealthy Behaviors 43

Rescued from the Struggle with Doubt 55

Rescued by an Angel 69

Rescued Before the Storm 79

Rescued from the Shame of Singleness 91

Works Cited.. 105

Rescued by Bitter Water

As women, we so often get caught up in the many hats we have to wear that oftentimes we become emotionally exhausted and frustrated. Our responsibilities of being mothers, daughters, friends, leaders, co-workers, wives, partners, volunteers, bill payers, soccer mom, therapist, and homemakers that we forget the devil hates us and will do anything to keep us from walking in victory. But we're not merely frustrated.

As a whole, we're also incredibly stressed, drowning in self-doubt, and filled with anxiety. No matter our demographic, many of us also feel ashamed of our messy lives and inability to "keep up," isolated and unsure of who we can trust, and guilty that we can't give our families more of what they deserve. It is no wonder that women are becoming bitter to a certain extent.

Today, for most women they are not the *Leave it to Beaver* mom. I dare say many of us have to leave our homes on a daily basis, drop the kids off at daycare, because we are expected to build careers, be exceptional parents, stay fit, eat healthy, practice self-care, and hold the awareness of so many things that our mothers never even thought about, such as food sensitivities, school options, internet safety, emotional wellness, and sustainability. It's a wonder we are not beating our heads against a brick wall somewhere. Most women have all of these responsibilities with very little assistance from their spouses.

It can make us bitter not at those we love, but at life itself. We begin to reflect on the what-ifs of our lives. *What if I were still single? What if I did not get married? What if I only had one child? What if I had finished school, college? What if I had married someone else?* What many of us do not realize is the enemy sabotages our minds by planting seeds of discontent. It's one of his favorite weapons for women. Do you want to know why? Because it leads to bitterness. Then bitterness leads to hate and hate leads to violence or self-destruction,

1

which is his ultimate joy to destroy us. But God knew we would face these challenges, so let's look at the children of Israel because their journey can help us as women. In the book of Exodus, we read:

"And when they came to Marah, they could not drink of the waters of Marah, for they were bitter; therefore the name of it was called Marah." **Exodus 15:23**

Marah means—bitter.

When the children of Israel came to Marah, the water is bitter and they cannot drink it. The main thing to note about the Israelites is that they are God's chosen; they are redeemed people. The wilderness journey starts the day they were washed by the blood of the lamb and received their deliverance. Their path has been mapped out and marked by God Himself, and they are following it. Something else that is important to know about them is that they are *Not* out of the will of God. They are at Marah because God sent them there.

I have learned as a wife, mother, teacher, and just by being a woman that bitter experiences will come to the child of God after our conversion. I do not know how to explain it, but I know it happens. It is puzzling and perplexing. How many times have you heard this from a new convert: Why did God let this happen to me?

When we read 1 Peter 4:12 he tells us, *Beloved, think it not strange concerning the fiery trial which is to test you, as though some strange thing happened unto you.*

What I notice when I read this text is that Peter did not say something was going to happen; he said it in the present tense. He wrote that it is happening to you new and old converts. Being a Christian does not make us immune to life's trials and tribulations. You will have trouble. Trials do come. But still it's our nature to ask the inevitable question again—why would a good and loving God allow us to go through things like the death of a child, disease and injury to ourselves and our loved ones, financial hardships, worry, and fear?

Now I cannot explain it, but I can give you this word of comfort—God is not punishing you, and you do not need to ask God why He let this happen. God is educating you; He is preparing you for something.

Every person reading this will have a Marah. I've had mine and I'm sure it won't be the last time. Can I ask you, have you come to yours yet? If you have not, it is out there; you can't outrun Marah. Many of you have been there. Some of you are there right now.

But I have good news for you—Marah is just a camping ground. It only requires a tent; it's not a permanent destination. Marah is not a beautiful brick home in the suburbs; it is not a place to live—it's just a camping ground. God brings you to Marah, but guess what? He will not leave you at Marah. But He will bring you there. On this journey called life, every believer has to stop at Marah, the place of bitter water.

When I got out of college, it was hard finding a job. As a graduate, it was my belief that with a bachelor's degree finding a job would be easy. I took a job at Rich's working in their portrait studio. I really thought I would have the opportunity to advance from the portrait studio. I wanted my name tag to have manager under it. After about three months, it became extremely clear that was not the case, and after the realization of that set in, I became bitter. Then my life went from being bitter to depressed, completely unmotivated—you name it. I just had absolutely no motivation. Nothing I did mattered; I was just running out the clock until I could find something new and it was driving me insane and affecting me personally. I was becoming mean and bitter and I hated it.

One day, my pastor asked me if I was still looking for a new job. I told him I was, and he asked me—is the bitterness over? I responded, yes. The revelation I received from him was that bitterness was blocking me from getting a job.

I stayed in that job for two years. I was a new convert then (just like the children of Israel), and I questioned God (just like the children of Israel). I did not know it then, but that job was my Marah. The only reason I had to stay for two years was because I was angry for being at my Marah. But if you ask me now, if God was in that experience, my answer would be a resounding, Yes! I met a young lady working at Rich's who is now a member of my church. I was able to be a witness for God on that job. Many of the people I met on a daily basis heard me talk about the goodness of my Lord Jesus Christ.

So, I can say to you that this bitter young lady working at Rich's and not being able to find employment anywhere else for two years was there because God led me to Marah. But He did not leave me there. At some point in each of our lives, we all come to a place of Marah. When we get there, a choice must be made, bitter or better; it's up to you. We cannot choose what comes to us, but we can choose how we respond to it, and that is what determines whether we become bitter or better. He led me down there so He could use me as a new

convert. I realized that much later as I matured in Christ, and He did use me. Today one of those people who heard me talk about God's love, walks into my church with her family to worship God. Marah was for my benefit and not my defeat.

God always brings His own down to the bitter waters of Marah so that He can use them later on. This is a very important lesson: You must not look to man; you look to God. Keep your eyes on Christ. We become frustrated with disappointments and the bitter experiences that we have as God's children! And there are times when the world tumbles in on us and we wonder what to do next. This means there was no pleasure no joy, no strength, no refreshment, from or in that circumstance. Can I get an Amen?

When I became unhappy with my job, or when you got angry with your boss, wanted to divorce your husband, there were two possible responses you could have made, either murmur and complain or trust God and move on. I was too young at the time to know what to do but now I'm older and I've been to and through Marah. What I should have done, was praise God and worship God, not because of the situation but in spite of it.

My question is: What do you do with your Marahs? How do you handle them? Let's look at what the children of Israel did. *And the people murmured against Moses, saying, What shall we drink?*

Don't judge them because how many times when an experience became bitter have you and I said, "Lord, why? Why do You let this happen to me? Why do these bitter waters have to be in my life? Why did my marriage have to end? Why did infidelity have to be my cup of tea? Why did my child have to be an addict? Why did my spouse have to die? Why did I have to lose my parent? Why did I have to battle cancer?"

Notice what Moses did in **Exodus 15:25,** "*And he cried unto the LORD; and the LORD showed him a tree, which when he had cast into the waters, the waters were made sweet: there he made for them a statute and an ordinance, and there he tested them.*"

Wasn't it that simple? He prayed to God. All this tells me is that we need to trust God. Paul says in **Romans 5:3-4,** "*We glory in tribulations, also knowing that tribulation worketh patience, and patience, experience, and experience hope.*"

How many times have we gotten frustrated and gotten upset needlessly over these kinds of situations. Some have spent the best part of their lives in frustration, while all they needed to do was pray. If someone were to tell me all of their problems and I told them I knew how they could solve them, they would be waiting for my response. I can see them now, crawling for the answer, "Please tell me," and when I tell them, "You need to pray," they would tell me or look at me like I am crazy. Then there are some people who say, "I trust in God," but the reality is that their life is far from trusting, and instead they are worrying. It makes for a lot of negative grumbling and trying to figure out life's problems on their own.

When we trust God, it's more than just opening our mouths to say it; we must not be anxious about the outcome. I've seen people with this cool demeanor on the outside but in reality, they are all over the place. They are like the duck which on the outside seems to glide across the water, but under the waters its feet are moving vigorously. Trusting God is just like that duck, God is moving but you have to believe it by the faith He has given us.

I believe that God has a divine purpose for us. He may not send trials, but He may permit them. What we must believe with everything in our soul is that when trials come, and as I stated earlier they will, they must find us still trusting and leaning on the Lord. The benefit will be a blessing, not only to you, but to those around you. It will give you a promotion that also gives you a new responsibility in the kingdom of God. We are also telling God use me for your Kingdom Lord because I'm an overcomer, but when trials come, we are begging God to remove them. How can you say, "*I can do all things through Christ Jesus who strengthens me,*" if there is no trial coming your way? If things are not against you, how will you know God is with you. There are times when God will test you. The obedience test was given to Abraham way back in the beginning of the Bible in the Book of Genesis.

Most of you have heard of this test. God asked Abraham to put his son Isaac on an altar and then asked him to take a knife and kill his own son. As we all know, Abraham went as far as to actually tie his son down to the altar and had the knife in his hand ready to strike down on him to take his life, when all of a sudden God sends an angel down in the nick of time to stop him.

How many of us could actually pass such an extreme test today, especially in the type of world we now live in where you would be immediately persecuted if you even tried to do such a thing.

This test will actually be hard for many to pass. The reason being is due to all of the material and lustful things that are out there competing for our time and attention. These material things could cause our flesh to act up, and once our flesh has been riled up, it will do everything it can to try and get its own way, even if it means disobeying God.

God knows where your jugular veins and weak spots are on these kinds of tests. Therefore, He allows tests to target some of your weak and vulnerable spots, just like He did with Abraham by asking him to sacrifice his son Isaac.

God may ask you to give something or someone up. He may ask you to give up the job you are currently working at, or the person you are currently dating, as this person may not be the one that He has personally picked out to be your mate.

But whatever God may be asking you to do for Him, realize that this is an obedience test being sent your way and that you must fully obey the Lord with whatever He will be asking you to do for Him. If you do not obey His specific directive, and you choose to follow your own desires on these kinds of issues, then God will not be able to use you in the specific calling that He has set up for your life.

If you can't or won't obey God with this specific command, then God will question and doubt your ability to fully obey Him further on down the road with anything else that He may be asking you to do for Him. Peter says in **1 Peter 4:12,** "*Beloved, do not be amazed and bewildered at the fiery ordeal which is taking place to test your quality, as though something strange (unusual and alien to you and your position) were befalling you.*"

You know how Paul lived a life of strength? He had a thorn in the flesh, and he prayed to God and the Lord said, "*My grace is sufficient for thee, for in your weakness lies my strength.*" God has a purpose for our lives. He has chosen us to fellowship with Him in His kingdom, which will be for eternity. What a prospect! Life's a journey and sometimes may be a difficult one; there may be experiences of disillusionment and disappointment. Changes happen in all of our lives. One day the sun is shining and things seem to be all going in our favor and yet the very next day something happens that rocks our world. The question is, how do we handle these experiences when they come? Sometimes they are brief and sometimes they last for extended periods. The bottom line is that they will come. We are all affected by the changes that happen in our lives.

Recognition of and yielding to God's will is the one thing that enables us to recognize God's hand in every circumstance of life. The deciding factor is are you bitter, or are you better? You and I must accept the fact that the Marah experiences of life will come to us all. **Proverbs 14:10** states that, *"Each heart knows its own bitterness."* But there is One who has trodden the path before us—and His name is Jesus. It was Jesus who faced the ultimate *"Marah"* of life, for it was at the Cross that all the bitterness of sin was heaped upon Him. We can take the story we've been considering as a faint picture, an illustration of what Jesus did in coming to Earth.

Ladies, we do not want to be like Naomi by blaming God, and have to repent later. Here is the danger we all face— blaming God for our bitter waters. When we begin to blame God for our bitter waters, then bitterness begins to set into our own lives, Naomi had identified herself with her bitter waters. But God told Moses to cut a tree and make it sweet. Maybe you are like Naomi when she returned to her city repenting for the decision she took, and said call me not Naomi but call me Mara, for the Almighty has dealt very bitterly with me. But she had to eat her own words. When she bounced on her knee and held in her bosom, the child of Ruth and Boaz and the joy of her old age, she was glad that the neighbors did not change her name to Mara. Don't call yourself Mara, but remember the name God has given you. What is your name?

It may make you a little uncomfortable, but I have to give you the whole Bible and the big picture. **Deuteronomy 8:2 states,** *"Remember how the Lord your God led you all the way in the desert forty years, to humble you and to test you in order to know what was in your heart, whether or not you would keep his commands."* We must come to expect that there will be things that happen in our lives which will test us beyond our own strength. In fact, we may learn the ultimate lesson of life and that is God made this world. He controls it, and everything finally will work out together for our good.

I must admit that I never thought I'd forgive the person who infiltrated my life, my family and sanity. Now, this is not to say, I would suggest we go to dinner. But I had to decide to eliminate Marah and move to Elim. I had to choose not to be problem-focused but solution-oriented. I had to put my ill-treatment behind me with the help of God. To some of you this might seem like a no-brainer, but in fact it may not be that easy to relinquish your "superior" position of righteous victimhood.

Sometimes we have to ask ourselves these questions? Did the person who hurt me really consciously intend to treat me maliciously? Did they really have a personal vendetta against you? Or was it self-interest—that they, were centered on their own particular needs and desires, that they were oblivious to your own? I had to realize that even if the other person had been guilty of intentionally hurting me for no reason other than their own perverse satisfaction, it still made sense to forgive them.

My bitterness caused me far more harm than it did them. Because they were probably at Six Flags enjoying themselves. So, remember this Marah may be satisfying for a moment but after a while the bitterness will destroy you. Marahs will be there, but never forget there is Christ in the journey in the form of a tree. That will make your way sweet and He will bring you to Elim and give you rest. I hope and pray that we may learn and apply this area of truth as well.

God grant us the faith to follow You and to not only trust You as our Savior, but to follow You as our Lord. Teach us to walk in the wilderness and to follow You on this journey.

Digging Deeper

Don't be afraid to share and discuss your responses, but remember to discuss in love.

The story ends on a high note. **Verse 27**, *"Then they came to Elim."* It wasn't the Promised Land, but it was a place of rest and refreshment. There were springs of water for the people to quench their thirst; there were palm trees to provide nourishment and shade. When the Israelites had their minor crisis at Marah, they did not realize that the oasis at Elim was only some seven miles away. If only they'd known it was but a couple of hours' walking distance, they may not have made so much fuss. This is usually the case with God's dealings with us. Yes, there are difficulties, but times of comfort and peace are seldom far away. *Once we've gone to God first, then we can share with others our concerns about bitterness.*

What obstacle, relationship or situation seems insurmountable? Have you considered your disposition as you deal with it?

_____

_____

_____

_____

_____

How does this story encourage or challenge you? Does it make you want to seek God for guidance? Have you prayed about it?

_____

_____

_____

_____

_____

_____

_____

What is the meaning of bitter water in the Bible? What does it mean in your life? What has your bitter experience been like in your spiritual walk?

_____

_____

_____

_____

The people were asking God, "What are we going to drink?" when they found the waters of Marah were bitter. How would you phrase a similar question in your life?

Lord,

_____

_____

_____

_____

Take a moment to cry out to God. Bring Him your thirst, your hunger for justice, problems with leaders, your healing, or whatever is causing you to complain or be bitter. Write you prayer here.

_____

_____

_____

_____

Journal about your journey to and through a place called Marah and your impending arrival or arrival in Elim, your place of rest.

_____

_____

_____

_____

_____

_____

Chapter 1

Rescued by the Power of Prayer

In the prologue of *Rescue Me,* we are introduced to an intercessory prayer group that has been organized at Greater Community. I'm sure many of us have heard of intercessory prayer even if we have not done it ourselves. It is feasible to say that many of our lives have been affected because of the prayers of others on our behalf. In *Rescue Me*, I wanted to illustrate the fact that sometimes we need the help and prayers of others. Intercessory prayer is not the same as prayers for yourself, nor is it for your own guidance, or any personal matter, or any overwhelming generality. *So, what is it?*

What I'm about to say will probably draw some raised eyebrows, but it's true nonetheless. Intercession is not just praying for someone else's needs. Intercession is praying with the sincere desire and real hope that God will step in and act for the positive advancement of someone else. It is an amazing blessing when we set aside all of our needs and desires to trust God for someone else. It is trusting God without a shadow of doubt to act, to deliver, to change a situation even if it's not in the manner or timing that we were seeking. Scripture tells us that when we say prayers of intercession, we are building bridges between God and the people for whom we pray.

Remember, this isn't just a prayer, it's a deliberate action. It isn't just saying words, it's a construction project. In *1 Timothy 2:1-2*, Paul writes:

"Therefore, I exhort first of all that supplications, prayers, intercessions, and giving of thanks be made for all men, for kings and all who are in authority, that we may lead a quiet and peaceable life in all godliness and reverence."

Because Jesus has done the work of intercession and still intercedes for us with the Father, and because the Holy Spirit also intercedes for us, helping us unburden ourselves, we can now intercede for others. The Lord Jesus and the Holy Spirit have built bridges to God that we may crossover, so that we, too, can be in that bridge-building business. We have the incredible privilege of building a span from heaven to earth, from God to the person for whom we are praying.

Let's imagine you were the person that Greater Community had to develop a prayer chain for because you did not know the danger you were about to encounter. Maxine used the power of intercessory when she began to pray for Keenan and William. It was evident to her that they both needed covering because William hadn't been walking with the Lord as closely as he should have been. She was concerned that he would make a wrong decision about his life as well as his son's. We know from the book, *Rescue Me*, that she was concerned about him being drawn into the wrong crowd and straying into some dark areas, and she wanted to intercede for him.

In the Prologue, we can read about how this spirit of intercession began at Greater Community.

'*Lady Destiny stressed to each of them to be as invisible as possible outside the walls of the church. She wanted their praying to become a part of the background never taking any of the glory from God. It worked because every time someone new joined, they understood that their mission was purely a work of God and not for self-glory.*

The song playing on Mother Solomon's cell phone in the wee hours of the morning had alerted her that Lady Destiny needed the intercessors. After talking to her and giving her a few brief details, she made the first call. Mother Thomas made the second call to Minister Cassie. They knew others like Deacon Benson and Deacon Wilson, Destiny's father, would soon be joining them followed by many others who would bombard heaven on behalf of one of their own or someone who needed their prayers.

12

Tonight, they were bombarding heaven for a sweet child who had been one of the original members in their small group. She had been the youngest of the group. After her conversation with Lady Destiny, Mother Solomon's heart was heavy, and the tears that were soaking the front of her nightgown would not stop. She was old enough and wise enough not to question God, but the pain in her heart was real. For now, all she could do was trust God and pray. If they weren't vigilant in prayer, Maxine would be dead by the end of the night.'

Maxine's never once thought she would need the hand of God to move so quickly on her behalf. But this is true with most of us, in all honesty it has happened to me. I have experienced the struggle of wanting something to happen so bad and fast that I became impatience for God to unfold His plans. I love the way God works with all of us but I especially love the way he uses women. Have you ever taken the time to research the powerful women of the Bible? There are many of all ages who stood strong operating in their God–given calling. You may not know it but you are a woman of destiny and power.

Let's look at a few examples that may enable you to see yourself. For those of you who are mothers and have had to make tremendous sacrifices, let's look at *Jochebed*. By merit of her good deeds, she gave birth to the three leaders of the Exodus generation: Moses, Aaron, and Miriam. It was *Jochebed* who intervened on behalf of her son Moses. As mothers we always watch over our young and she was no different. It was because of her motherly protection that Moses was later used as the deliverer of Israel (*Exodus 2*).

Then it was Moses' wife (*no surprise there*), *Zipporah*, who saved his life when God was going to punish him for his refusal to follow a simple command (*Exodus 4:24-26*). *Queen Esther* and Mordecai were given Haman's estate. They were honored with royal garments and a decree was written to protect all Jews. *Esther's* bravery gave the opportunity for the Jewish people to defend themselves from what would have been utter annihilation. *Ruth's* refusal to return to her own people because of her dedication to her mother-in-law, *Naomi,* led to the on-going line of the Messiah (***Ruth 4:18-22)***. *Rahab* was

instrumental in the victory of Israel over Jericho. *Mary* carried God's Son in her womb.

I believe prepared women are dynamic women. This is seen in Destiny as she prepares the intercessory prayer group but it is also shown throughout *Rescue Me*. In life, we never know when the bridegroom is coming so as women we need to be ready at all times. Maybe, you are preparing for something that seems to be far off. The best advice that I can give is for all of us to be ready. In *Matthew 25* a story is told of five women who were *"anticipating"* a bridegroom's arrival. Once he came, the wedding party would begin! Five of the women *"prepared"* ahead of time by bringing oil with them so they could light their lamps when the bridegroom arrived; five brought no oil. When the bridegroom was close, the prepared women lit their lamps, while the others hurried out to buy oil.

In life we rarely have time to prepare for the unexpected, so when and if it does happen, wouldn't it be wise to be prepared? Destiny was preparing for the day when a call would come in for serious and fervent prayer that would be needed for someone in or out of their ministry. When we are interceding for others we are literally throwing down all of our weaknesses as we stand before God in all of His strength on the behalf of someone who does not even know we are holding them up in God's strength because our own weakness was casted down at his feet.

The Bible has many cases of people standing up for others before God. The most striking example is *Abraham*. He took the initiative to step forward before God on behalf of his neighbors in Sodom and its area. *Moses* also stepped in when God was angry, standing in the gap in the most literal sense—offering his own life for that of his nation. *Isaiah* prayed with *King Hezekiah* to save the nation from defeat and destruction at the hands of Assyria, and the armies were suddenly turned back (*Isaiah 36-39)*. *Nehemiah* prayed to God to bring about the rebuilding of Jerusalem and of his people.

The one trait I see in each of these men is compassion. The motivation that caused each of them to act was compassion. The only reason Lady Destiny

Wheeler wanted an intercessory prayer team was her compassion. Destiny loved the people of Greater Community; she loved the culture that had been built in their ministry. It was her faith that caused her to take the step of faith, which was balanced by her love of God and it burned in her so much that she dared to believe others felt and loved as much as she did.

The Holy Spirit will never allow you to pray alone. It is the leading of the Holy Spirit that urges, pushes you to pray for that mother and her three children; it was the Holy Spirit who whispered in your ear to pray for the young man sitting in front of you during the altar call; it was the Holy Spirit who told you to pray for your boss after he fired you. Just because you may be praying at home with no one else around, you are never alone. Romans tells us this: *"Jesus does our praying in and for us, making prayer out of our wordless sighs, our aching groans. He knows us far better than we know ourselves."* **Romans 8:27 MSG**

So, Maxine comes to God with this crushing weight on her heart because she loves William and Keenan, and she's deeply concerned for him and some of the choices he had been making. However, she feels helpless to change his course of action. *What would you do if you were Maxine? How do you intercede for him?*

First, you take hold of God. Because when the disciples came to Jesus and asked Him how to pray, He told them, essentially: *"After this manner therefore pray ye: Our Father which art in heaven, Hallowed be thy name."* **Matthew 6:9**

The one thing the disciples asked Jesus for was a tutorial on prayer. They never asked how to preach but they did want to know how to pray according to **Luke 11:2-4**, where Jesus taught them the Lord's prayer. This was different from Matthew's version but the same prayer.

Maxine's version might be something like this: *"Father, I thank You that You made a bridge for me. I thank You for saving me by grace through faith, through the Lord Jesus Christ. I thank You, God, that You are an all-knowing, all-powerful God. You are a loving God and a merciful God, and I praise You for Your greatness... for Your wisdom... for Your kindness to me..."*

You take hold of God by acknowledging who He is and by thanking Him and praising Him for all He has done. Second, she would take hold of William and Keenan.

You say, *"Lord, You know the weight on my heart today. I'm bringing William and Keenan to You right now. I ask You to protect him. I ask You, dear Father, to take away all the evil influences of friends around him who are trying to lead him in a wrong direction. I ask You, Lord, even to replace those friends with other friends who know You and love You and will bring William to You. You know this deep concern on my heart, Lord, I can't hide it from You. So, I bring it to You, in Jesus' name."*

In *Rescue Me,* Maxine takes hold of God in one hand and takes hold of William and Keenan in the other hand, and become a bridge between them. She stands in the gap for those she cares about. She prays, *"God, I'm bringing William to You, and I'm asking for a miracle in his life. I'm asking that the Holy Spirit will go to William and convict him of the way he has been living. I know that this is Your will, Father, and that right now I am praying in Your will."*

I have heard lots of prayers like hers at my church, and they have always moved me. How much more must they move our Father in Heaven, who loves us dearly! Desperate and soul-stirring prayers like hers result in answers.

When God is sought in desperation, He responds—even in hopeless situations. So, she prayed for William, and didn't give up on him, no matter what. She continued to pray until there is an intersection between William and God, until William finally runs into God's arms and God's way becomes his way.

Jesus Himself said it: "Pray always, and don't give up." The reason any of us can do this is because Jesus has first made a bridge for us. The Lord's prayer was a starter kit. It was giving them a starting point but you must grow in your prayer life beyond the Lord's prayer.

When the disciples came to Jesus and asked Him how to pray, He told them, essentially: The first thing you do is to honor God. You say, Our Father in Heaven, Hallowed be Your name. (**Matthew 6:9**)

Your version might be something like this:

"Father, I thank You that You made a bridge for me. I thank You for saving me by grace through faith, through the Lord Jesus Christ. I thank You, God, that You are an all-knowing, all-powerful God. You are a loving God and a merciful God, and I praise You for Your greatness, wisdom, and kindness to me."

You take hold of God by acknowledging who He is and by thanking Him and praising Him for all He has done.

You might say, like Maxine did for William, *"Lord, You know the weight on my heart today. I'm bringing _____ to You right now. I ask You to heal him or her. I ask You, dear Father, to take away all the evil influences of friends around him or her who are doubting that you can heal. I ask You, Lord, even to replace those friends with other friends who know You and love You and will bring_____ to You and teach him or her to trust You. You know this deep concern on my heart, Lord, I can't hide it from You. So, I bring it to You, in Jesus' name."*

Do you see how that works?

You take hold of God in one hand and take hold of who you want to pray for in the other hand, and you become a bridge between them.

We do not know what we should pray, but the Holy Spirit makes a bridge and gives us His prayer agenda. He knows the will of God and helps us make a connection between our will and what God wants. The word *helps* means that two parties mutually bear a burden. The Holy Spirit wants to help you carry your burdens to God, and prayer is simply the transference of a burden. We are not created to be burden bearers; we are created to take our burdens to Jesus and leave them there with the Spirit's help.

Intercessory prayer is not cold, detached, or impersonal. It's building a bridge from heaven to earth. At times of inward dryness and depression, praying for others' salvation, sanctification, and prosperity can bring your soul into a place of renewal. Prayer unites us with the purpose of God and lays itself out to secure those purposes. Not only is prayer the medium of supply and support, but it is a compassionate agent through which the mercy of God has an overflow. Prayer influences God greatly.

Why are intercessors needed? Intercessors are needed because God has things He needs to do on the earth. He has a will, a plan, and a purpose for everything and everybody on this planet! But you know what? He needs you and I to pray so He can accomplish that will. **Psalm 115:16** tells us why: *"The heaven, even the heavens, are the Lord's; but the earth He has given to the children of men."*

We must ask God for what we desire. That "permission from us" comes when we PRAY earnestly and ask Him to do things. And that, my friend, is the start of intercession. If we want to see revivals, manifestations, and miracles we must intercede. We see this clearly in **Ezekiel 22:30-31**, which says: *"So I sought for a man among them who would make a wall, and stand in the gap before Me on behalf of the land, that I should not destroy it; but I found no one. Therefore I have poured out My indignation on them; I have consumed them with the fire of My wrath; and I have recompensed their deeds on their own heads,' says the Lord God."* Dare to be an intercessor it will change your life and change the world.

Digging Deeper

Don't be afraid to share and discuss your responses, but remember to discuss in love.

Maybe you're thinking right now about someone you know who needs Jesus but whom you've quit praying for. Let's stop right now and pray for that friend or family member! We can be the bridge between God and that person!

Who are you praying for today? Who did you pray for this week? Was it someone you knew or was it a complete stranger?

_____

_____

_____

_____

_____

_____

_____

After you prayed was there a sense of peace in your spirit? Write your thoughts.

_____

_____

_____

_____

Think about the scene in the prologue when Maxine was in the hospital. When your mind is not clear, just as Maxine's mind was in that hospital room, the Spirit stepped in for her. It was the Holy Spirit who urged the church to pray on her behalf. **Romans 8:26** says, *"Likewise the Spirit also helpeth our infirmities: for we know not what we should pray for as we ought: but the Spirit itself maketh intercession for us with groanings which cannot be uttered."*

Oftentimes prayer changes as needs change so our prayers are forever changing. As an intercessor, you must be prayerful about the needs of others. It is important to seek God for what to pray for. Just because we desire for them to be delivered immediately, we must remember that the Lord might be using the burden to prepare them to do something for God. *Think about a time when you were struggling or even in a dark place.*

Did you take the time to listen to what the Spirit of the Lord was saying, and pray that God's will be done? Write about the decision you made.

_____

_____

_____

_____

Matthew 6:5-6, *"And when thou prayest, thou shalt not be as the hypocrites are: for they love to pray standing in the synagogues and in the corners of the streets, that they may be seen of men. Verily I say unto you, they have their reward. But thou, when thou prayest, enter into thy closet, and when thou hast shut thy door, pray to thy Father which is in secret; and thy Father which seeth in secret shall reward thee openly."*

We must stay focused when we are praying for others; they must be our first concern. Think about that one person you have been praying for? Write the name below.

_____

List specific concerns you must focus on during you intercessory for them.

_____

_____

_____

_____

There is always going to be a time for prayer and a time to act. So, don't be surprised if the Spirit starts tugging on your heart to take some sort of action about a matter you're praying about. You may be the answer God sends into that person's life. The Spirit might be calling you to be more than a bystander. Be ready for it. Be open to it. When you intercede in prayer, bring your knowledge, gifts, abilities, attention and energies before God and say, "use these, if that's what it takes to set this right" for my brother or sister.

Write about a time when the only thing you could do in the situation was pray and act.

_____

_____

_____

_____

_____

_____

_____

Let's consider several intercessors throughout the Bible:
Who was the intercessor for the Israelites at Sinai? **Exodus 32:7-14**

_____

_____

_____

_____

_____

Who interceded for Nabal when he foolishly offended David? **1 Samuel 25**

_____

_____

_____

_____

_____

Who intercedes for us even now? **Hebrews 7:23-25**

_____

_____

_____

_____

_____

Journal about how intercession has changed your life.

_____

_____

_____
_____
_____
_____
_____
_____
_____

Chapter 2

Rescued During the Darkness of Depression

If being a happy person is a moral responsibility, how much more so is being a joyful person? Happiness skims the surface; joy is rooted in eternity. We are commanded to be joyful not merely for our own benefit but for the benefit of everyone else in our lives!

The Bible is filled with faith, hope, and love. I believe they are there to teach us when all is right with the world and when all seems to be wrong with the world. These words are necessary for us to have a vibrant faith. Although different from each other, these three words (*faith, hope, and love*) are related.

Think of each of them as siblings. Hope says, "*I know things will work out; I just don't know how or when!*" Then Faith says, "*Things have already worked out,*" although she has not yet seen it come to pass. Love being the oldest speaks with the wisdom of the eldest saying, "*Even if they don't work out, even if I don't understand what's going on, nothing can separate me from the affection God has for me!*"

Choosing defiant joy in the midst of heartbreak is not an impossible choice. In chapter 31, Maxine talks about her parents and the grief her mother held on to in her heart. These are her thoughts.

"I remember doing that with my mother for my father," Maxine said. *"I didn't want to at first; it was so depressing and sad during those first years,"* Maxine admitted. *"But my grandmother believed it was important to remember even if it hurt, and now I am happy that we did it."*

"Are you okay talking about this Maxine because we can stop," he stated noticing some sweat on her forehead. They both fell silent, but his thoughts were everywhere. Maxine was twenty-six now, so she had been without both her parents for a total of ten years. For a young adult, Maxine appeared well adjusted. In fact, William thought she was one of the kindest people he'd ever met.

Maxine was happy that she had gotten over the anger she carried in her heart at God when she lost her father. She had been a Daddy's girl. Her grandmother told her that anger would only make her an unhappy girl growing up. This was because of what Maxine witnessed after her father's death and her mother's behavior during her grieving process. Her mother realized that she was scaring her young daughter to the point of alienating her. When Maxine had desperately needed her, she had terrified her.

But Maxine remembered that her mom had taken her to church, and the pastor talked about forgiveness and how much it hurts the person who is angry. So, she told her mom that if they both prayed together before going to bed and asked God to take care of her daddy, maybe her daddy would hear them.

Her mom's response was just, "Yes, Maxine, maybe he will."

In *Rescue Me*, we are made aware of Maxine's mother and her bout with grief dealing with the death of her husband. We are also told about Maxine's depths of defeat, discouragement, despair and depression. Maxine and her mother, Dorothy, have been brought low by the burdens of life. They both have difficulty trying to decipher their relationship with God. Maxine's father was gone. But Maxine was alive and well and grieving the loss of her father in her own way. She had suddenly lost her dad and then, in the days that followed, watched her mother slip away from her as well. Her sorrow was magnified; her fear left unchecked. Joy was out of her reach.

Can you remember that overwhelmingly sad feeling when you learned that someone you loved died? What about the guilt and embarrassment you felt after your biggest failure was exposed? Do you ever think about the time you were facing the biggest problem in your life and thinking that it was impossible to fix? If you think really hard you probably can remember that time, as a little kid, when someone held you under the swimming pool too long, and you thought you were going to drown. Roll all of those emotions into one, carry them around with you every day from the time you wake up until the time you fall asleep, and you will begin to understand depression.

Maxine was desperate when she told her mother that they should both pray for her father together. She was saying, *"I am alive. I need you. Do you still love me?"*

It was at that moment her mother began to live again. It's amazing to see how the kingdom of God is filled with paradoxes, surprises. We set out to find joy for ourselves, only to discover the greater joys waiting for us when we live for others. The reason I bring all this up is simply this: Quite often we cannot find reason enough to choose joy and pursue joy for ourselves. But perhaps we can find new strength when we realize how much it matters to God and to those around us.

Maxine had always seen God's hands in the life of her family. She believed that God would take care of her family if they kept the faith, had a balance of hope against hope, and demonstrated the love of God. When this didn't happen, after her father died, she felt as though she and her faith in God were a failure. Maxine and her mother are a clear portrait of a people who are dealing with depression.

When you experience depression, your entire world is seen only through the lens of sadness, hopelessness, mourning, loss, emptiness, grief, pain, anger, frustration, guilt, and death. Death is always there, looming and lurking making you say things like: *"I can't live another minute like this. Death has to be better than this. The people around me would be better off if I wasn't here to hurt them. I can't do this anymore. This is never going to get any better."*

Depression puts you in a cyclical prison cell. It's like my dog, Tyco, use to do chasing his own tail: *"I am depressed. Because I'm depressed, I can't do what I need to do. This makes me feel like a failure. That makes me depressed. Because I'm depressed, I can't do what I need to do. This makes me feel like a failure. That makes me depressed."* After all of that chasing you are dizzy, confused and tired.

25

I can remember when one of my dear friends in the ministry was going through a battle that had their mind trapped in a place full of darkness. In a personal Bible study over the phone, I took them through the story of Elijah found in *1 Kings 19:1-4*.

Elijah stands as one of the greatest men in the Old Testament. God used him in his generation to bring revival to a nation. He saw God do miraculous wonders just because he asked Him to. God shut off the rain at Elijah's request and sent it again when he prayed. God fed him with ravens. God multiplied meal and oil for him and a widow's family. God used Elijah to raise a dead boy back to life. God sent fire down from Heaven when this great man of God prayed. He was truly a powerful preacher of the Word of God.

In chapter 19, we are confronted with Elijah's humanity. We are given startling evidence of this by the words James used concerning Elijah, *"Elias was a man subject to like passions as we are." James 5:17*

When I took the time to discuss this chapter with that dear member I mentioned earlier, it was important for her to see Elijah as a man who pushed himself beyond his physical and emotional limits. Why was this important? Because sometimes as Christians we push ourselves beyond our own physical and emotional limits. In actuality it is something we do often. In this 19th chapter, Elijah is in a period of depression. More than any other chapter in the story of Elijah, we are given a clear picture of what happens to him, while at the same time, although we may be shocked, we are also helped.

Many of us are shocked when we realize that great men and women go through periods of deep, dark depression. For instance, Winston Churchill said, *"Depression followed me around like a black dog all of my life."*

In the 1800s, there was a young lawyer who suffered from deep depression. It got to the point that his friends did everything they could to protect him from himself. They hid all of his razors and knives, because of their concern for his well-being. Later he penned these word, *"I am now the most miserable man living. Whether I shall be better, I cannot tell. I awfully forebode I shall not."* You may be surprise to know that this young lawyer was our 16th president of the United States. His name was Abraham Lincoln.

Even the great preacher, Charles Spurgeon, went through periods of depression. History tells us that there were times when Spurgeon would be so depressed that he would refuse to leave his home to go to church. On more than one occasion, his deacons had to come and physically carry their pastor to the pulpit.

I understand that some of these accounts shock us, but they also can serve as a way to help us. They remind us that depression is a common experience. It is something that often happens in life. What I am actually trying to tell you is that, if you go through a time of depression, you are not alone. Let's look at some of these facts concerning depression.

Depression affects all classes, races, ages, groups and genders of people.

This year 17.6 million Americans will deal with some form of depression.

One out of every 5 Americans can expect to deal with depression in their lifetime.

The rate of clinical depression among women is twice that of men. Statistics remind us that one person out of every seven in this very room will need some form of professional help in dealing with depression in their lifetime.

The National Institute of Mental Health estimated that depression costs this nation between $30-$44 billion in 1990 alone (Center for Mental Health Services, 1996).

In addition to that, over 2 million work days are lost each year due to depression (Center for Mental Health Services, 1996).

Depression is the leading cause of alcoholism, drug abuse, and other addictions.

Untreated depression is the number one cause of suicide.

Depression is not something to mess with! If you are dealing with depression, get the help you need!

What you don't want to do is allow what people say, old prejudices, and spiritual stupidity to stand in your way of getting the help you need.

One fact to remember is that all depression is bad. Depression is the body's natural reaction to shock (Auerbach, 2003). When a time of grief, stress, frustration, or illness occurs, the brain will release chemicals that will serve to numb the mind and body. This is like a shock absorber. However, there are times when the brain and its chemicals become so out of balance that clinical depression may occur. Professionals say that a period of depression lasting over 2 weeks should be considered serious and needs treatment (Dom, De WB, Hulstijn, & Sabbe, 2007).

In this episode of *As Elijah's World Turns*, great things have just happened on Mount Carmel, and Ahab has returned home to his wife Jezebel. She has been anxious all day waiting for the news of how her prophets have come out victoriously. No doubt, she has seen the fire from a distance and now she sees the rain. In her sinister mind, no one could have done these things but her god Baal. But when her jelly back husband comes home he is defeated and probably begins to cry as he tells the boss the news.

She is angry, *"Do not tell me that I left you with my prophets and you allowed all of them to be killed?"* When she hears this, she is infuriated! She probably throws clay pots at the walls and turns over chairs in the room where they are currently standing. Then she tells him loudly, *"I shall take matters into my own hands!"* She turns to her husband and shouts at him, *"Elijah must die!"*

Have you ever met a woman who is so domineering that her husband is afraid to come home? Well ole' Jez was that kind of domineering woman. Ahab had no say so in this matter. She had all of the decisions. Jezebel did not believe in the leadership of her husband. She took his power and used it the way she wanted to in regards to ruling. I don't know but women like this will scheme and intimidate their husbands into submission. Ahab had no backbone; he was afraid to stand up to his own wife. He was the King who allowed his wife to sit on his throne. What a sad picture of leadership we have in this saga! Jezebel was the puppet master working the strings and Ahab was the puppet moving at her will.

What neither Ahab or his wife wants to admit is that our God is greater! Baal had no dominance in this encounter. Can't you see Ahab calling on the name of Baal but to no avail? They even began to cut themselves thinking that their blood had power. But we know the only blood that works according to the Word of God is the blood of Jesus, *"...that at that time you were without Christ, being aliens from the commonwealth of Israel and strangers from the covenants of promise, having no hope and without God in the world. But now in Christ Jesus you who once were far off have been brought near by the blood of Christ."* **Ephesians 2:12-13**

We are told that it got so bad that at noon Elijah began to taunt them, saying, "Shout louder, for he is a god!" What Elijah knew that Ahab did not was that there was only going to be one God to show up on that mountain and He was Jehovah. Ahab should have been on his face before the God of all gods but he refused to surrender and repent. Still trying to play God cheap, Ahab did not give God credit but instead he credited Elijah for the victory.

When Jezebel hears this news about Elijah, she sends him a warning that she is going to have him put to death. Elijah runs fearing for his life. This was the same man who had to deal with a brook being dried up, had an encounter with a woman with an empty barrel, raised a dead boy, took on the prophets of Baal, dealt with a lack of rain and through all of that God provided. God closed the heavens, God replenished the barrel, God raised the boy, God consumed the sacrifice, and finally God enabled Elijah to destroy the false prophets. The question would be why would Elijah run from Jezebel to Jezreel?

This is just some interesting facts for you the reader to know. Elijah runs due south almost 125 miles. I used to run and can I tell you that getting a mile run in took some time, at least for me. Ahab had to have supernatural endurance to run that many miles. Can you believe he actually left Israel and ran all the way to the southern border of Judah? It's one thing to run, but to run from a woman who had just been defeated was truly unusual. This behavior by all accounts is irrational, but that is one of the effects of depression on the human mind. It causes the sufferer to think in ways that are not normal. Depressed people often

do things that defy logic and description. Yet, to them, their actions make perfect sense.

There are many people who find themselves vacillating between their sadness and their joys. In **Psalm 42,** we have a psalmist who pours out his pain and one minute he is up and the next he is brought down real low. I have been there, have you? Really? Have you ever been in the pits of hell in your mind?

Elijah leaves his servant at Beersheba and goes alone into the wilderness. When we see him again he is under a juniper tree, throws in the towel and asks God to take his life. Poor old Elijah has reached rock bottom. Elijah displayed some characteristics in this event that show us that his thinking was anything but rational. Elijah is at the end of himself and it shows. When these characteristics begin to appear in our lives, we need to take a close look at the condition of our heart. It's then that we need to start looking for some warning signs. Elijah exemplified some signs that we can examine. He cuts himself off from those close to him.

It's in verse *3: "And when he saw that, he arose, and went for his life, and came to Beersheba, which belongeth to Judah, and left his servant there."* This caused him to feel alone. Another sign would be his irrational thinking. Elijah never thought about the 7,000 who had not bowed to Baal in Israel, and he never went to them for assistance.

One of the worst effects of a depressed spirit is the desire to separate oneself from everyone. Many people who become discouraged have a tendency to develop an *"I'm all alone"* or a *"Nobody understands"* mentality. If these feelings are allowed to go on unhindered, the pessimistic person begins to think that he or she is the only person in the world who is right. It becomes, *"me against them."* That is a sad, lonely place to be! You see this kind of thinking in the church all the time. A person will become discouraged and will drop out of church saying, *"No one understands me. I just don't fit in."* What they are doing is projecting their own feelings of hopelessness onto those around them.

Sometimes we are looking for a scapegoat to place blame because we hate to look within. *Have you ever looked in the mirror and not recognized the person looking back at you? What ever happened to that person? Did you lose them somewhere along life's road? Was it a bad relationship? A divorce? Some addiction? Unforgiveness?* So, we find ourselves backing away from the one place we need to be with other believers who support us and love us. We need fellowship!

It's so important according to **Hebrews 10:25,** *Not forsaking the assembling of ourselves together, as the manner of some is; but exhorting one another: and so much the more, as ye see the day approaching.* Not everyone will be able to understand what you are going through, but you will have those who are spiritually in tune with you to pray for and with you. You need balcony friends who will lift you up and not basement friends to pull you down.

It's easy for us to take our eyes off God but you can't keep your eyes on what you can't see. So often we take our eyes off the Lord because of troublesome co-workers, marital difficulties, rude people, unfair situations, life's problems, et cetera. The lesson is simple—keep your eyes on the Lord and you won't go under!

When we find ourselves frustrated, discouraged, and angry because of people—we need to focus our eyes on the Word of God and the Lord Jesus Christ. It is quite easy to lose sight of our Christian beliefs, when overshadowed with adversity and grief. It can be overwhelming at times. People can be so cruel. We respond like the Israelites who grumbled about food only days after their exodus from Egypt.

The next step to a downward spiral is when we stop interceding for others and start requesting help for ourselves. It's what Elijah did in verse 4. This was the first time Elijah had prayed for himself. He had forgotten that he was the prophet to Israel. His attention is full of himself. When any of us as Christians become self-conscious and it dominates our thinking, check yourself because you are not yourself! You are in trouble spiritually.

We can't get to the place that we feel like, *"Life is hopeless."* It's what happened to Elijah in verse 4. He said, in effect, *"I've had it! I quit!"* Do you know what he did? He sat down and he gave up. Don't act like you don't know what it feels like because all of us have had that experience. You remember the time

31

that your whole life seemed to be going down the drain because the man you loved didn't love you. I remember my first love. To my way of thinking he was the perfect young man for me. At the time, love had nothing to do with maturity, and everything to do with the fantasy of being in love.

Have you ever asked yourself, *"Why do I love this person? Was it because we work well together, love each other's personalities, and could truly build a life together?"* With my first love, I knew from the beginning that we were perfect for each other, and before we started dating I knew I wanted to spend the rest of my life with him. But as time would have it, we broke up. He was the first man to not be faithful to me. I was devastated. My heart was broken. My whole world was collapsing around me and I felt that life would never be the same.

All of us have felt that way about love or being in love. Do you remember bawling your eyes out—that ugly, unattractive, can't breathe properly, snotty-nosed, kind of sobbing? You needed them to make everything better. Young love always exists in an uncomplicated world before joint bank accounts, shared belongings, in-laws, kids' sports, and social studies projects. Young love is powerful. It's irrational. It's all-consuming. It's addictive. And it leaves an indelible scar when it combusts. Sometimes it sends us into a tailspin.

As long as we can remember that there is hope, we can make it through. May we never forget that God is still on the throne, and no matter how bad things become, God is in control! He knows where we are and what we are facing. He will see us through! As long as there is a God in Heaven, there is hope for us. Elijah gave up on life, on ministry and on God.

Elijah claimed that he wanted to die, verse 4. *But he himself went a day's journey into the wilderness, and came and sat down under a juniper tree: and he requested for himself that he might die; and said, It is enough; now, O Lord, take away my life; for I am not better than my fathers.* Many people who are depressed have these types of thoughts. However, most are irrational just like Elijah's. If he really wanted to die, why didn't he just stay in Jezreel and let Jezebel take care of it for him? Again, this is just more evidence that he is thinking very irrationally.

All of these things that Elijah said and did are typical of depressed individuals. In fact, it might be helpful to you for me to list some of the symptoms of depression.

Lethargy - Everything seems like it's too much trouble to do.

Disturbed Sleep:

(Early waking, difficulty getting to sleep, waking up tired after a normal night's sleep)

Loss of Interest in Usual Activities

Feelings of Guilt, Worthlessness and Hopelessness

Lack of Concentration

Irritability

Exhaustion

Lack of Sexual Desire

Sensation of Utter Despair

Sense of the Hopelessness and Uselessness of Everything

Fear of Death

Phobias

Obsessive Behavior

Permanent Sense of Anxiety

Feelings of Wanting to Cry, but Inability to do so

Bouts of Uncontrollable Crying

Thoughts of Suicide

Changes in Appetite and Weight

There are many other symptoms. This is not a definitive list by any means.

If several of these things are true about your life, then you may need to seek some sort of help. Do not be ashamed to get the help you need, because depression can literally ruin your life.

Do you actually think that you are above having episodes of discouragement and depression? It can happen to any of us! If you have recognized a tendency in your own life to be depressed and discouraged, let me invite you to bring your need to the Lord Jesus. He wants and waits to help you. Remember what

He said, **Matthew 11:28**, *"Come to me, all you who are weary and burdened, and I will give you rest."* **Hebrews 13:5**, *"I will never leave you nor forsake you."* **1 Peter 5:7**, *"Casting all your care upon Him, for He cares for you."*

I will leave you with this thought: Your depression is not a sin, and it may not always be the result of sin! However, to allow yourself to wallow in it is a sin! If you see signs of depression in your life seek the help you need.

Let me remind all of you that Jesus is bigger, stronger, and Most High over everything. When we read this story about the naked man at the beach, the demon of depression recognized and yielded to the authority of Jesus. Jesus is bigger than depression. Whether you personally hunted down your depression or it stalks and then tries to ambush you, Jesus can set you free again.

Depression will make you think that you are a nobody. You, my sister or brother, have been made by God. **Genesis 1:26** says, *"Let us make human beings in our image, make them reflecting our nature."*

Go ahead and say this now! *"I am somebody?"* It's easy to feel anything but important when the corporation you work for sees you as a number; the boyfriend you adore treats you like cattle; your ex with all of his nagging and baggage takes your energy; or the old age that is ravishing your body takes your dignity. You have the nerve to say you are somebody? Hardly.

When you struggle with that question, remember this promise of God: *You were created by God, in God's image, for God's glory.* Don't let depression or anything steal who God created you to be. God spoke in **Genesis 1:26** and said, *"Let Us make human beings in Our image, make them reflecting Our nature so they can be responsible for the fish in the sea, the birds in the air, the cattle, and, yes, Earth itself, and every animal that moves on the face of Earth."*

Certainly, God's perfect will for Maxine would have been for her to have stood and to have faith by renewing her devotion to the Lord God. God knew that Maxine had expended all of her physical energy and was worn out. *What Maxine needed was a break! God knew that and allowed her to rest.*

What God did for Maxine was exactly what God did for Elijah in **1 Kings 19:5-8** and what he did for King David in **Psalm 13, 32, 71,** and **22**. God ministers through compassion. Not only did the Lord feed Elijah and allow him to rest, He also dealt with him directly. It is a blessing to see how the Lord spoke to this discouraged and defeated prophet. It teaches us that the Lord has compassion on the fearful, the fallen and the foolish.

God orchestrated Maxine's life by allowing her to have more than she could ever imagine. God cared for Maxine with gentleness. There are no sermons, no lectures, no threats, no reproaches and no rebukes. The Lord simply *"touches"* Maxine's life, meets her need and gently speaks to her. ***Verse 6*** *also shows us the condition of Elijah's heart.*

Notice that when the Lord appears to William, there is no repentance for the past, no gratitude for the present and no burden for the future. William is a man in desperate need of a personal revival! Yet, the Lord is so gentle with this wayward man! I think too many of God's children have the impression that God is standing over them with a cosmic baseball bat, just waiting for them to make a mistake so He can bash them with it. This is not so with our God. **Isaiah 30:18** says, *"And therefore will the Lord wait, that he may be gracious unto you, and therefore will he be exalted, that he may have mercy upon you: for the Lord is a God of judgment: blessed are all they that wait for him."*

William is not by himself because we all have fallen short of the glory of our God. We have all sinned and deserve God's judgment. God, the Father, sent His only Son to satisfy the judgment for those of us who believe in Him. Jesus, the creator and eternal Son of God, who lived a sinless life, loves us so much that He died for our sins, taking the punishment that we deserve, was buried, and rose from the dead according to the Bible. If you truly believe and trust this in your heart, receiving Jesus alone as your Savior, declaring, "that Jesus is Lord," you will be saved from judgment and spend eternity with God in heaven. Many claim to believe in heaven and in hell, yet, unfortunately, show little concern over their eternal destiny. We are far more concerned about this life than the next, yet we know that eternity is endless. **Revelation 22:5** describes eternity as being *"forever and ever"* (*"And there shall be no night*

there; and they need no candle, neither light of the sun; for the Lord God giveth them light: and they shall reign for ever and ever.").

Digging Deeper

Don't be afraid to share and discuss your responses, but remember to discuss in love.

God used Elijah to do some truly extraordinary things for Him. Go back through this study and list at least six things God used Elijah to do. After you list his accomplishments list at least six extraordinary things you've seen God do in your life.

_____

_____

_____

_____

_____

What signs of depression did Elijah exhibit in this chapter of his life? Have you seen any of these signs in your own life? If so explain.

_____

_____

_____

_____

Why was Elijah depressed? Thinking about his depression have you ever been where he is in your life?

_____

_____

_____

When was the last time you had difficulty maintaining the excitement of a spiritual experience or commitment? How did it change your life?

_____

_____

_____

_____

_____

In what situations do you feel that you are the only Christian around?

_____

_____

_____

_____

As Christians, our spirits will live forever, but our bodies and emotions are human. We get hungry, tired, discouraged and sick. We must take care to rest and maintain balance in our lives if we are to continue to be useful to God and His mission. Also, when we are with godly Christian friends who care about us and pray for us, we are more energized and supported than when we try to live life by ourselves. God was patient with His man. He knew that Elijah needed a partner, so He sent him to find and become a mentor to a young man named Elisha.

Who was Elisha according to **2 Kings 2:1-25?**

_____

_____

_____

_____

How could Elisha help the older prophet? How can you assist others or yourself?

_____

_____

_____

Elijah began to teach and train Elisha to be his successor. *Who are you helping to grow in their Christian faith?*

_____

_____

_____

Each of us sometimes has spiritual highs or mountaintop experiences. What really counts is what we do when we come back down to earth. Elijah rested, ate, talked to and even complained to God. God then sent him to train a new prophet. Giving our time to help others be successful lifts our spirits and makes us feel more productive.

Do you get enough sleep? ○ *Yes* ○ *No*

Do you eat properly and maintain good health? ○ *Yes* ○ *No*

Do you give your time to train or disciple someone else? ○ *Yes* ○ *No*

Who in your life needs a mentor or partner? Explain why?

_____

_____

_____

_____

_____

Are you in the middle of heartbreak? If so write about it and try to explain why?

_____

_____

_____

_____

Are you unhappy? If so write why?

_____

_____

_____

_____

What do those around you need from you?

_____

_____

_____

_____

_____

Can you find any examples of how God intervened in your life to give you a reprieve from your life, the memories, and sadness of your past life?

_____

_____

_____

_____

Just as a reminder: God never intended our bodies to run like we force them to! You and I should never be guilty of laziness, but we should get the rest our bodies need. *When we are rested, we will accomplish more for God than we will if we are exhausted physically.* Discuss a time when you were physically exhausted.

_____

_____

_____

_____

When life is hard or disappointing, it's easy to get stuck in a negative mind-set, especially when we feel as if life should be one way but instead it's another way entirely and we don't like it one bit. We feel stuck when it seems we've done everything possible to bring about change in our lives yet nothing seems to change at all.

In **1 Kings 19: 5-6,** *God considered _____ need for rest. Where did he have to go in order to receive it? Where do you go for your help? Are you finding the healing you need?*

_____

_____

_____

When we are rested, we will accomplish more for God than we will if we are exhausted physically. Is this true for you?

_____

_____

_____

_____

Remember, even the Lord Jesus took time to rest. **Mark 6:31,** *"And he said unto them, Come ye yourselves apart into a desert place, and rest a while: for there were many coming and going, and they had no leisure so much as to eat."* *When we are in a time of discouragement, depression, or doubt, we will find that the Lord knows just how to meet our need. Often, He will deal with a symptom before He deals with the problem. Why? So that we might be in a position to listen more clearly!*

How did God orchestrate this in Maxine's life? Has God had to deal with your symptoms before He dealt with your problem?

_____
_____
_____
_____
_____

How did God orchestrate it your own life?

_____
_____
_____
_____
_____
_____
_____
_____
_____
_____
_____
_____
_____

In **1 Kings 19:5** *had the Lord tried to reason with Elijah when he was exhausted, hungry and depressed, nothing would have been accomplished. And as he lay and slept under a juniper tree, behold, then an angel touched him, and said unto him, Arise and eat.* **Job 10:1,** *"My soul is weary of my life; I will leave my complaint upon myself; I will speak in the bitterness of my soul."*

How can you deal with the bitterness that has been right under the surface of your life? Have you acknowledged it or are still trying to hide it—hoping not to break down? Journal about your discovery.

_____

_____

_____

_____

_____

Chapter 3

Rescued from Unhealthy Behaviors

aving *Comparison* issues can cast you into a pit. It will eventually yank you down so deep and keep you captive in a pit so deep that the muddy sidewalls will not allow you to scale the walls back to safety. It shuts doors that seem as if they cannot be reopened. It leaves you in a cave that screams adjectives like: *alluring, angelic, appealing, beauteous, bewitching, charming, classy, cute, dazzling, delicate, delightful, divine, elegant, enticing, excellent, exquisite, fair, fascinating, fine, foxy, good-looking, gorgeous, graceful, grand, handsome, ideal, lovely, magnificent, marvelous, nice, pleasing,* and finally *pretty.* It's toxic talk that weighs down on the person who feels as if they cannot measure up. But it is a lie, and *Comparison* is devious and sinister.

But don't worry. God would never leave his child in a pit of deception. He couldn't. I truly believe that our detachment from God causes us to find ourselves more isolated as individuals in our relationships, and communities. That's because we're looking for our self-worth in the wrong places, and for the wrong reasons. The way we measure our glory is in how it is reflected back to us in the approval and admiration of others. We figure the more approval and admiration, the brighter our glory, and the greater our self-esteem. But this is not true. It was Maxine's thoughts about herself that influenced her opinion and those death words cut straight through to her heart and they resonated with her more than she knew.

Maxine had scars left behind by the comparison trap. They had cut deep for years, ever since her own childhood. And she understood the rejection she

felt from her only male friend. When you grow in this understanding of who you are in Christ, you can let go of wrong thinking or any rejection from others. You can rise above the *"blues"* of depression and say with the Psalmist, "*Why are you so downcast O my soul? Why so disturbed within me? For I will yet praise Him – my Savior and my Lord.*" **Psalm 42:5**.

When you believe that you are valuable in God's sight—you will start acting like it. You will assert yourself and set boundaries so people will treat you with the dignity someone made in God's image deserves. Maybe you have been looking for your identity in the approval of others. Maybe you've been looking for it in your performance and role at work or at home. Now is the time to transition from finding your identity in what you do to finding out who you are in Christ!

In chapter 8, Maxine allows the reader to see her spiritual personality. In this sample from the chapter let's discuss who she is as God's daughter. *'Her saving grace had been getting involved in her grandmother's church, Greater Community. Pastor Wheeler's teaching had helped her develop a different philosophy which she still cherished. 'The shell may be pleasing to the eye...but it's what the shell encompasses that truly matters. Because as time moves on, the shell may fade, but what's inside lives on forever, praise God!'*

Look at her now—any female in the Seattle area would consider this to be a dream job. William was six feet plus of masculine perfection. He was also several years older than her. Maxine knew she'd never be his type or have the opportunity to have a higher paying job that would pay enough to help pay off her student loans.

You have not promised me that this will be perfect, but You have vowed to stay with me. I can see only William and Keenan's faces, Lord. I can hear Keenan's sweet voice. If it does not last, give me direction. If I am to stay, guide my heart. I'm ashamed that I didn't ask ahead of time, but if this is a family of believers, I'm happy about that. I'll miss working at Mama's, but I trust that You will expand my world. Give me friends, Lord, and help me to be a blessing to those who know me. Touch Mr. Kennedy's heart as he raises his son in Your word. Help him to trust You at home and in his business. I pray for his father and Anna. Touch his heart. Help all of us to walk with our hands in Yours.

Maxine prayed on this fashion several minutes before she got out of her car. She did not know what lay ahead, but she did know that whatever it was, her future was in God's sovereign hands. *"Just me and You Lord,"* she said, and a smile formed across her face.'

In the book of *Proverbs*, we are told about a woman who fears the Lord. **Proverbs 31:30**, *"Charm is deceitful and beauty is vain, but a woman who fears the Lord is to be praised."*

Now I believe that there are some things we need to recognize about Maxine and any woman who fears the Lord. A woman who fears the Lord needs to know how to fill the role she is placed in whether she is married or single. She should also inspire others, if she married then this should be her husband and children. As a single woman, she should inspire those around her or the people in her sphere of influence.

A woman who fears the Lord will not run away from God to satisfy her longings and relieve her anxieties. She will wait for the Lord. She will hope in God. She will stay close to the heart of God and trust in his promises. The prospect of departing into the way of sin will be too fearful to pursue; and the benefits of abiding in the shadow of the Almighty too glorious to forsake.

Oftentimes we don't want to think about it but our looks fade. This is a fact of life for everyone and including me. When I was a young girl, I couldn't imagine this happening but then slowly over time I saw one gray hair and then another. Then it seemed as if I could not keep my chin from drooping, then there were the wrinkles which began to appear. So, I had to admit it to myself, I was aging. Looks only go so far. They don't make us happier, wiser, or godly. They are literally only skin deep and have nothing whatsoever to do with having a meaningful life.

Maxine suffered from low self-esteem stemming from her battle with weight—which caused her to negative self-talk. It is any inner dialogue you have with yourself that may be limiting your ability to believe in yourself and your

talents in order to reach your potential. It is any thought that diminishes you and your ability to make positive changes in your life or your confidence in your ability to do so. Let's go back to that passage in *chapter 8* of *Rescue Me*.

'Thinking back, she had never had that happened before. She attributed that to her body size. Even as a little girl in grade school, she had been called 'fat.' The adolescent years were no better. As a teenager, she had gotten 'used to' not having clothes fit and all of the other things that went along with being a plus size teenager. Nothing had prepared her for the heartbreak she was dealt with her first male crush, Alfonso. At the time, she thought they were friends. They'd studied together and spent time hanging out at her house, eating her grandmother's chocolate chip cookies and studying. She had the biggest crush on him. Alfonso wasn't the cutest guy, but he never seemed to mind her weight. They talked for hours and hours about classes and anything to do with sports. Then one night, they were at the library, and Alfonso looked at her and said the worst thing she'd ever had anyone say to her.

He'd said with all sincerity. "With your personality Maxine, all you would need is a nicer body and guys would be falling all over you." She had just sat there and stared at him, not believing or wanting to believe what she'd just heard. As a "fat girl" she just shrugged it off and chalked it up to how her life would be. It took her years to realize that if others chose to not like her because of her exterior, they were the ones missing out on a good thing. She attributed her weight gain to her grieving, especially after losing both of her parents in such a short amount of time. The counselor at her school told her grandmother that she was suffering from a deep depression, and her weight continued to pile on.

Self-esteem refers to a person's beliefs about their own worth and value. It also has to do with the feelings people experience that follow from their sense of worthiness or unworthiness. Self-esteem is important because it heavily influences people's choices and decisions.

"You are the light of the world. A city on a hill cannot be hidden. Neither do people light a lamp and put it under a bowl. Instead they put it on its stand, and it gives light to everyone in the house. In the same way, let your light shine before men,

that they may see your good deeds and praise your Father in heaven." **Matthew 5:14-16.**

In other words, concentrate now on living fully for Christ. In living fully for Christ, you will find strength and hope for living, new meaning for your life, and a new identity—an eternal perspective when you feel troubled by the changes in your life. Your faith can bring you hope in the midst of the circumstances and people around you and a joy even when life disappoints you because Jesus loves you and will carry you through.

Digging Deeper

Don't be afraid to share and discuss your responses, but remember to discuss in love.

A woman who fears the Lord has to make choices and decisions. But they must be wise choices. *Do we live for ourselves or do we live for the Lord and what He has asked us to do? Do we make our looks an idol in our lives (because if we do, we will be devastated when we find that first gray hair) or do we make the Lord our God and know that His plan for our lives is perfect? Write your response and share your response with the group.*

_____

_____

_____

_____

_____

_____

We see beautiful women everywhere. They are on our television and advertisements all over the place. They show off their bodies and try to entice men but what happens to them as they lose their beauty? They have built their lives and security on their looks which fade over time and then what do they have? Have they built up their marriages and families and their relationship with Christ—the things that last or have they built their lives upon sand?

...but a woman that feareth the Lord, she shall be praised.

This is what it all comes down to, women. We are called to fear the Lord. This means that we live for only His approval. We do what He has commanded for us to do since we owe Him our lives. Our homes are built upon His Word. We train our children in His ways. We rejoice in Him always! A woman who fears the Lord will not run away from God to satisfy her longings and relieve her anxieties. She will wait for the Lord. She will hope in God. She will stay close to the heart of God and trust in his promises.

The prospect of departing into the way of sin will be too fearful to pursue; and the benefits of abiding in the shadow of the Almighty too glorious to forsake.

It is the fear of the Lord that makes us beautiful on the inside and adorning ourselves with a meek and quiet spirit while living in submission to our husbands. The fear of the Lord urges us to grow in wisdom since we must be able to navigate clearly in this evil generation that tells us that what is right is wrong and what is wrong is right.

The only way to grow in wisdom is to be in His Word and learn from the One where all wisdom comes from. The days that we live in are very unstable but the Lord is not; for He is the same yesterday, today, and always. Measure everything you hear and read with His Word. He is our stability and knowing Him and living for Him is all that matters in the end.

Each of us is a spirit son or daughter of God just as Maxine, and we enter mortality to gain a physical body. Our physical body is a gift from God and ultimately will become a resurrected body.

The Apostle Paul describes the body as the temple of God in **1 Corinthians 3:16-17**, "*Do you not know that you are the temple of God and that the Spirit of God dwells in you? If anyone defiles the temple of God, God will destroy him. For the temple of God is holy, which temple you are.*"

1 Corinthians 6:19-20, "*What? know ye not that your body is the temple of the Holy Ghost which is in you, which ye have of God, and ye are not your own? For ye are bought with a price: therefore glorify God in your body, and in your spirit, which are God's.*"

The one thing that I wanted for Maxine in *Rescue Me* was to portray her as a woman who struggled with weight but was conscious of the necessity of staying healthy. Each of us should try to keep our body healthy by eating properly, exercising regularly, seeking competent medical help, and living the Word. This will help us in our work, family, and spiritual life.

What are you doing to stay healthy?

_____

_____

_____

_____

Have you ever negative self-talk? If you have why?

_____

_____

_____

_____

_____

Do you need to improve any unhealthy habits?

_____

_____

_____

_____

_____

If so, what do you need to do to succeed in making these changes?

_____

_____

_____

_____

_____

In what ways is your body a temple of God? **1 Corinthians 3:16**?

_____

_____

_____

_____

_____

What can you do to respect and care for this temple?

_____

_____

_____

_____

_____

In what ways can your physical health affect your spiritual health?

_____
_____
_____
_____
_____

Addiction to any substance enslaves not only the physical body but the spirit as well. As a Christian how should we handle addiction? **1 Corinthians 10:13-14**, *"There hath no temptation taken you but such as is common to man: but God is faithful, who will not suffer you to be tempted above that ye are able; but will with the temptation also make a way to escape, that ye may be able to bear it. Wherefore, my dearly beloved, flee from idolatry."*

How does this scripture encourage you if you have an addiction?

_____
_____
_____
_____
_____

Lives are filled with various forms of temptations. It's our forgiving God's words where people can find the encouragement and strength to overcome these cravings that may defile the temple that God has given us. **2 Corinthians 5:17**, *"Therefore if any man be in Christ, he is a new creature: old things are passed away; behold, all things are become new."* Think back to the time when you were a new Christian similar to Maxine. You were trying to be a better you. Maxine was trying to keep a temple healthy but her image of herself were conflicted by the words of others in her earlier years.

Do you think William was frustrated with his obsession about body image? Did he do right by Maxine and her healthy lifestyle even when he could not understand Maxine's faith in believing she could accomplish her goal? How do you encourage yourself when others don't support you? Does it stop you from moving forward?

_____

_____

_____

_____

William doesn't wish to condemn Maxine, but he wants her to take better care of herself. What advice would you give Maxine?

_____

_____

_____

_____

_____

_____

_____

_____

Sometimes the critique of others can be very helpful in identifying areas that we need to change, but we are blind to. I try to honestly assess those critiques through prayer and ask God's Spirit to point out the things that are true, and then put aside those things that I know are false. Journal about some of your identified areas below.

_____

_____

_____

_____

_____

_____

Are you too critical of the child (*you*) that God made? Do you think that He could have done a few things better? **Isaiah 43:4,** tells us that we are *"precious and honored"* in His sight. The Creator of the universe chose every part of your body, just as He chose where to put each star in the sky. He thinks you are incredibly special! Journal your thoughts below.

_____

_____

_____

_____

_____

_____

Chapter 4

Rescued from the Struggle with Doubt

Have you ever been visited by an unwanted guest? I have and her name is *Miss Doubt*. She's the neighbor that always shows up when you least expect her. She's the obnoxious guest that gets on your last nerves. Just when you were all prepared for a weekend of peace and relaxation...just when you have tossed the shoes that have your feet barking all day into the closet and climbed into your warm bubble bath—just when you adjusted your bath pillow and leaned your head back while closing your eyes, it happens—you hear that annoying voice interrupting your thoughts.

"Hey, Sylvia. Can I get a few minutes of your time? I've got a few questions. I don't mean to be obnoxious, Sylvia, but how can you believe that a big ole' God could ever care about you? Why do you spend so much time in church? Does it really take all of that to be a Christian? There are so many other things you could be doing with your life. What makes you think that you are even good enough to get into Heaven?"

Do you know someone like that? Constantly pestering you. Asking the same question over and over again. Pestering you. Criticizing all your decisions. She'll pull the rug out from under you and watch you stumble. All the while she's laughing because her whole motive is not to convince you, but to confuse you. She never comes to you with a solution; all she does is ask more questions.

Like Maxine, we are often conflicted by the decisions we've made or the consequences that may come from those decisions. It's tempting to think that many of us will reach a point in our lives where we'll be forced to question all that we believe, and then after this struggle we'll never doubt

again. But the truth is that our beliefs are tested every day. It happens when you make a decision on your own without the opportunity to discuss with those who could be most affected by that decision.

What about the time your car broke down on the day your husband used your only credit card to buy a new suit for his job interview the next day? In my 58 years, I've learned a few things and the more I've sought to know and understand God, the more I'm certain that doubts have been essential to my maturity as a believer. If I wanted to have strong faith, then I had to be wise enough to allow my doubts to stand as I worked through them instead of trying to ignore them.

Have you ever had thoughts that were fixed on certain questions? The ones that erodes trust and keep repeating in your mind when you feel abandoned—*Why hasn't Jesus come? Has something terrible happened? Why hasn't He even sent word? Does He no longer care? Has He no real control anyway? Why?*

Psalm 143:5-8, "*I remember the days of long ago; I meditate on all Your works and consider what Your hands have done. I spread out my hands to You; I thirst for You like a parched land. Answer me quickly, LORD; my spirit fails. Do not hide Your face from me or I will be like those who go down to the pit. Let the morning bring me word of Your unfailing love, for I have put my trust in You.*"

In *Rescue Me,* William and Maxine both doubted God, which in turn caused them to doubt each other. It's contagious because our doubts can affect others around us especially if we let them flow out of our spirit into the atmosphere. *But it raises the question: why would God allow us to doubt to begin with? Why does He allow us to wrestle with deep questions about our life, our relationships, our prayer life, our current or past pain, and suffering?* Judging from what I see in Scripture, I'm convinced that God honors those who sincerely look for the truth, just like that boy's father who wanted to believe so badly that he asked God to help him overcome his unbelief (**Mark 9:21–24**). Maybe you can relate. You are like so many others who want to believe but feel like life has gotten in the way. In the passage from *Rescue Me* we see the struggle that Maxine is having stepping out on faith to trust God.

Maxine's stomach did a nervous somersault. "I must believe and I must trust you. My spirit says I can?"

Nagra studied her for just a moment. "You can and you have to believe. I don't blame you for being careful. As Kenyan women, we are taught early not to become involved in business with men. In our country, this refers to a mistress or girlfriend; one does not get involved in her lover's business. But as you have stated rather frankly, you are not a bibi, but a prayer warrior. Therefore, if you truly love William, then you are going to have to stop being so afraid. You must start acting like the strong woman William needs—or you will both lose everything God wants for the both you."

I told you that *Miss Doubt* is a big-mouthed, two-faced liar who deals from the bottom of the deck. Don't let her fool you. Though she may speak the current jargon, she is no newcomer. Her first seeds of doubt were taught to her by the master of doubt in the Garden of Eden. She was messing with Maxine's mind in *Rescue Me*.

Life isn't perfect. In spite of all the glossy photos we see in magazines or on Pinterest, life is often messy, chaotic, and confusing. In fact, life can feel unbearable sometimes. When we experience chronic pain, are forced to make tough decisions, face difficulties within our families, experience a fracture in a friendship, or even lose someone we love, our lives are thrown into a sea of turmoil. We become confused. We are plagued with doubt and fear. We may even lose sight of God within the swirling storm clouds. As Christians, we have the comfort of knowing that there is a calm amidst our storms. You can think of your messy life as a unique hurricane, and if that's the case, God is the eye of your storm. In God–the eye– there is nothing but peace. Although damaging winds and lightning may fly around you, there is calm in the arms of the Lord.

In the Gospel, we see Jesus on the Sea of Galilee with His disciples. In **Mark 4:35-41**, Jesus was resting as the group navigated toward their destination. A storm suddenly appeared and began raging before them, pounding their boat with angry waves. The disciples became afraid and sought Jesus, who calmly arose, rebuked the winds, and said to the waves, *"Quiet! Be still!"* As we know, the wind died down, and calm fell upon the sea once more. We may also remember what Jesus said to the disciples next in **Mark 4:40,** *"Why are you so afraid? Do you have no faith?"*

Like the disciples, we may not actively seek God when life is calm or ordinary. We often find ourselves scrambling toward Jesus in the midst of life's storms. In these storms, the Lord's mighty powers are revealed to us as He helps us endure what lies ahead. We can count on our God, who conquered death, the grave, and the power of Hell itself, to guard and protect us, no matter what type of trial comes our way.

"And when he got into the boat, his disciples followed him. And behold, there arose a great storm on the sea, so that the boat was being swamped by the waves; but he was asleep. And they went and woke him, saying, "Save us, Lord; we are perishing." And he said to them, "Why are you afraid, O you of little faith?" Then he rose and rebuked the winds and the sea, and there was a great calm. And the men marveled, saying, "What sort of man is this, that even winds and sea obey him?" **Matthew 8:23-27**

"*'Follow Me!'* he said, *'Follow Me!'* Look where that's gotten us!" Those are the words I imagine the disciples of Jesus saying in the middle of the Sea of Galilee as the worst storm they had ever seen began to violently throw their boat around.

The entire scene unfolds midway through the eighth chapter of Matthew's Gospel. Jesus has just finished telling each of them to, that is right, you guessed it— **"Follow Me."** To their credit, that is just what they do. They leave behind the world they have known to follow Him into a life they do NOT yet know. Beginning in **Matthew 8:23** we read the words, *"And when He got into the boat, His disciples followed Him."*

Now, I am sure they thought this would be a leisurely glide across a familiar sea. These guys were not rookies; many of them were seasoned fishermen. They had been on this sea hundreds, if not, thousands of times. However, this night would be very different.

In **verse 24**, the whole scene abruptly changes. *"And behold, there arose a great storm on the sea."*

Like something out of a movie, a storm, the likes of which they have never seen, cuts through the calm and throws everything into chaos. Sound familiar? Is this how storms seem to come up in your life? Yeah, me too. One minute it is calm, the next is chaos. As the story continues, it becomes clear that these seasoned seamen are totally overwhelmed. The words of **verse 24** graphically show this, *"so that the boat was being swamped by the waves."* That is a gentle way of saying that the boat is going down with them in it!

Now, where is Jesus in all of this? Wasn't He in the boat? What was He doing? Was He shouting out instructions? Was He calming everyone down? Was He joining in to keep the boat from capsizing? Nope. None of the above. The last four words of **verse 24** tell us simply, *"but He was asleep."* Did you read that? He is asleep!

The sky is dark, the wind is howling, rain is sideways and pouring down on them as wave after wave brings the boat up and then sends it crashing down. Wave after wave comes in what seems to be an endless succession and the little boat is taking on water. These Navy veterans are powerless to the storm's force. It is too big for them! All their experience and strength have yielded nothing. There is Jesus, we are told in Mark's Gospel, *"in the stern, asleep on a pillow."* Jesus could hardly get away for any rest.

The fact that He could sleep on a boat during a raging storm when the others feared they were about to drown, might indicate how tired He was at times. Even though the winds and the waves didn't awaken Jesus, the cries of his needy frightened disciples aroused Him to their aid. Jesus slept right through a storm. But the minute the cries of His fearful and fretting disciples reached His ears, He is awake and goes into action. This teaches us volumes about the Lord.

Even though a storm doesn't bother Him in the least, the cries of His people cause Him to spring to their side to help. Never doubt His love and care for you.

After Jesus had calmed the storm, He turned to them and said, *"Where is your faith?"* You cannot have great fear and great faith; they cannot coexist. When we have great faith, we will not have great fear, and when we have great fear, we will not have great faith. Now, these disciples had some faith, but it *was "little"* faith. They had faith enough to obey Jesus and take the boat out into the lake. When the storm hit, they had enough faith to go to Jesus and wake Him up. *Do you have that kind of faith or will you allow your doubt and fears to keep you from going to the Master?*

Digging Deeper

Don't be afraid to share and discuss your responses, but remember to discuss in love.

This journey called life can be frustrating. Do you believe what has happened to you over the last week, month, or year has helped you? Has it built your confidence and developed your character?

_____

_____

_____

_____

_____

_____

_____

_____

_____

_____

_____

Sometimes we doubt that God cares about what we are going through. It's hard to believe that you have been anointed to go through your present situation. Perhaps it is your marriage, your children, or your health. Do you trust God that there is something you need to learn and develop from it? Can you be grateful even when doubt persists?

_____

_____

_____

_____

_____

_____

_____

A storm, the likes of which you have never known, has suddenly arisen in your life. It is fierce, and it is throwing you. Wave after wave crashes into every area of your little *"boat."* Waves of fear, worry, and pain. Oh sure, you have your *"ups"* where you know the Lord is in control, but then like the boat that day, down you go into despair—side to side, from this thought to that. As you read this, you have used all your energy in prayer, and it has not changed a thing. You feel like you are taking on water, and everything inside you says, *"You are going to drown, this storm is too big; it will be the end of you."* Oh, and Jesus is asleep.

Is it any surprise that once they have exhausted their own resources, they finally turn to Jesus for His help? Write about a time when this happened to you.

The story goes on to tell us that the disciples wake Jesus and say this, *"Save us!"* That is not all they say, for Mark's Gospel tells us they despairingly ask Him a question. They ask, *"Don't you care that we are going to die?"*

That is the question, isn't it? In the middle of your storm today, the one you are going through as you read this.

The question we end up asking is, *"Why aren't you helping us? Don't you care? Why are you asleep in my time of need? Why aren't you intervening? Why aren't we hearing anything from you? Don't you care about us?"*

Do you ever wonder if God cares? *What about when you received news that was devastating? How did you deal with it in that moment? Have you learned how to trust God with difficulties in your life?*

_____
_____
_____
_____
_____
_____
_____
_____
_____
_____

How has someone comforted you with God's love in the past or how have you corrected your own thinking when feeling alone and like no one cares?

_____
_____
_____
_____
_____
_____
_____
_____
_____
_____

You see, there was a purpose in this storm. It was not random happenstance. There is a purpose in your storm. In **verse 26** Jesus asks them, ***"Why are you afraid, O you of little faith?"*** He was essentially saying, *"Guys, what are you so worked up over?"* That is kind of an odd thing to say to them considering the circumstances, isn't it? It sure seems odd when He says it to you and me in the midst of our storm. However, He has actually put His finger RIGHT ON THE ISSUE; He is saying, *"Don't you trust Me?"* According to Jesus, it is just simple math; they are afraid = they do not trust Him.

Do you agree that it is a trust issue? Why?

_____
_____
_____
_____
_____
_____
_____
_____
_____

The disciples trusted Jesus in certain things just as you do. However, do they trust Him in this life-threatening situation? On that boat, they just do not know. They do not know if He is in control. They do not know if they are safe. They do not know if He can handle this. They do not know.
Are trust issues also control issues?

_____
_____
_____
_____
_____
_____
_____
_____
_____

You see, the disciples ask TWO questions in this story. We have already mentioned the first one, *"Don't you care?"* The second will come at the end of the story after He puts His hand out and calms the storm with a word (verse 26). That second question is: **"Who is this?"** You see, this storm did

64

more than cut through the calm of night; it cut through them. It revealed their weakness. It exposed their hearts and minds. It was masterfully used by the Master to teach them two truths: (1) He does care. (2) He was in control.

In truth, they had no reason to worry, no reason to fear. They were never actually in danger. You might ask: *"How can you say that?"* Because Jesus said it, *"Why did you fear?"* You see, He said to them as they got into that boat (something you would not know until you read the other Gospel's accounts of this story), *"Let us cross to the other side."* Guess what? They made it to the other side. They did not drown. They were ALWAYS going to make it to the other side. Always!

Discuss a time when you made it to the other side.

_____

_____

_____

_____

_____

_____

_____

_____

_____

_____

_____

_____

Jesus knew everything would be fine, and so He was asleep. *However, they did not know they would make it to the other side—did they? Yet, Jesus said it; Jesus was with them, and Jesus knew it. It becomes an issue of trust. What about you? You do not know everything that is going to happen, but you do know Him. Do you know that He cares? Do you know that He is with you? Do you know that He is good? That He is able? That He has a plan?* If you do not, He is going to prove it to you, through this storm you are in today.

Do you agree God cares? That He is with you? That He is good? That He is able? That He has a plan? In your own words discuss how you know God cares, and that He has a plan for you.

_____

_____

_____

_____

_____

_____

_____

_____

_____

_____

Perhaps He seems asleep? He is in control. **Perhaps He is silent?** He cares. **Perhaps He is not leading?** He has a plan. **Is it ever going to end?** He calmed it with a word. Trust Him. Trust Him. Trust Him.

One last thing we cannot miss in this story. In light of all this, we realize something; they could have been resting too. They could have been resting with Jesus. Instead, because they are unsure of Him, they are exhausted, doubting, and filled with debilitating fear! **Hebrews 4:9** tells us that, ***"There remains therefore a rest for the people of God, let us be careful to enter that rest."*** This rest, in the midst of a storm, comes from being sure about Jesus, who He is and that He cares.

Therefore, to summarize—this storm had a purpose. **Your storm has a purpose.** These are always our trouble struggles when we are in storms. Who is He really? Is He the all-powerful, all capable God that we have thought Him to be? Can He really be a healer? Can he really be Counselor? Can He really be the one who fixes marriages, gives hope, and has a plan? The question remains: *"Does He really care?"* Maybe you have asked: *"God I know that You are able, but I don't know if You WANT TO?" "Do You care about my situation? My STORM? DO You SEE what I am going through? Why are You so silent?"*

Can you think of a storm from your past that has already proven to have had value? Journal your thoughts about that storm.

_____

_____

_____

_____

_____

_____

It is through storms that we learn important life anchoring truths. **He is with us. He loves us deeply. He is in control. He has a plan. We are safe with Him.**

Chapter 5

Rescued by an Angel

Have you ever felt when you woke up on some mornings that there's something deeper you could be a part of? You feel the pull towards something but you can't exactly pin it down—it eludes you and frustrates you. I believe we all have these thoughts at some part in our life. We ask, *"What is my purpose in life?"*

Have you ever heard stories from writers, musicians, missionaries, pastors and people just like us who have felt their calling their entire lives; people all over the world who have pursued their passions from the moment they were out of their mother's womb. Deep down you wish you had this "unction" to pull you forward. In actuality, you do. All it takes is a little digging and sometimes some assistance from special agents sent to us by God to uncover the truth.

In *Rescue Me* there is a specific instance that the reader discovers that two of the characters in the novel are angels. The fastest way about how to find purpose in life is through the art of introspection—diving into the deeper essences of who you are to pull out the pieces to assemble the purpose puzzle. But there are some instances when you need help. Not that you do not have the desire to do it but you need help because sometimes uncovering your passion is like the work of a master sculptor. It's time-consuming like slowly chipping away at a stone to reveal the masterpiece underneath. Your life's purpose is this masterpiece, simply lurking beneath the surface waiting to be released.

Did you know that, Ms. Lenora and Nagra are not the only angels on assignment? Angels are active throughout the Old Testament for the sake of

God's people. That means there is even an angel assigned to you. Ministering spirits are angels who live right here on this earth with us. God says they encamp around us. These angels are helping all the time by ministering to us and removing hurts and cares. They know the objections, the strains, the pressures of life, and they are around to help us. Angels carry the very heartbeat of God, his love, his care, and his concern. Many times, God sends angels to minister to those in extreme times of pain, loss, or grief.

If you've ever sat at the bedside of a loved one who was at heaven's gates, whether you recognized it or not, you were surely in the presence of angels. Maybe one of your loved ones has spoken last words of seeing angels or light before being ushered straight into the presence of God. Maybe you just knew and you were comforted by the fact that they were seeing into a realm that we can't fully see, and it gave them peace and strength.

I've had that experience several times throughout my life when saying goodbye to loved ones. My Uncle Lewis would look out in the distance with an unexplainable peace and sometimes he would even smile. I would like to believe that an angel was preparing him for his journey home. It really gives us a picture of God's tender heart. He cares for His children enough to send us help in our greatest times of need and loss.

We see many accounts in the Bible of when God sends His messengers to provide comfort and to minister to those who are in need. When Elijah was afraid and running for his life in **1 Kings 19**, an angel appeared to him and provided food and water for his journey.

There are many examples in the Bible of when God sends an angel to give a specific message to an individual or people. In **Genesis 18**, God sent three men, messengers, to Abraham and Sarah to tell them that she would bear a son. He sent an angel to Sarah's servant Hagar in the desert, as she fled in **Genesis 16**, to give hope that she was not forgotten.

There are times when God sends angels to protect, guard, and fight for us. God tells us in **Psalm 91** that He would give angels charge concerning us to guard us in all our ways.

God sends angels to minister to those who hurt or need strength. God sent an angel to Daniel in the lion's den. **Daniel 6:22,** says that he shut the mouth of the lions so that no harm came to him who was found blameless before God. In the Garden of Gethsemane, as Jesus prayed and wrestled with what was to come, **Luke 22:43,** tells us that an angel appeared from heaven, *"strengthening him."*

Angels can be used by God to punish sin and to bring his judgment. **In 2 Kings 19,** King Hezekiah prayed boldly to God, asking for his help against their enemies. The Assyrians were known for the cruel way they treated their captives. *Verse 35 says,* "*That night, the angel of the Lord went out and put to death a hundred and eighty-five thousand men...*" In Revelation, we see specific times that God will give angels the charge to execute his judgment. **Revelation 12:7-9** tells us, "*Now war arose in heaven, Michael and his angels fighting against the dragon. And the dragon and his angels fought back, but he was defeated, and there was no longer any place for them in heaven. And the great dragon was thrown down, that ancient serpent, who is called the devil and Satan, the deceiver of the whole world—he was thrown down to the earth, and his angels were thrown down with him.*"

These are examples of angels sent by God to assist or strengthen His children. Not only do we read about this in the Old Testament, but we also see it in **Hebrews 1:14**. We read about God sending angels to minister for the sake of the people of Christ. This is one reason why Ms. Lenora Bessemer showed up for Maxine. But as you read Nagra, was there to guide and assist her in discovery of her purpose. There are people who have had encounters with angels in our world even today. Maybe some are aware of these angelic meetings. Maybe others have no idea they've walked or possibly talked with an angel.

We all need people to help us find the way. Both angels had a purpose and because of their voice, Maxine and William, found their own way to a better and fuller life discovering their God-given purpose. Angels are simply God's

servants who do His bidding for the sake of those who are on their way to heaven.

We're told in **Hebrews 13:2**, *"Do not forget to show hospitality to strangers, for by so doing some people have shown hospitality to angels without knowing it."* God is the same yesterday, today, and forever. Therefore, we can be confident that He still works in the same powerful ways, for He never changes.

Ultimately going to heaven is our goal. We are all trying to improve our life and live a meaningful life. Maxine felt the same way, especially after she was able to travel to Kenya. Sometimes, God will allow us to experience Him in a different way in order to find our way.

It was not until Maxine went to Kenya that she received the zest, more flavor, and more of the fullness of God. Maxine even declared that she desired to be a better person just as William did. Why? Was it because she or he wanted to wake up in the morning excited, jumping out of bed with a thirst for life that they hadn't felt? Or was it because they had just lost their way?

Your purpose can be your connection to something larger, something that will allow you to make your mark on the world to truly make a difference; a difference that will leave a legacy for your children and for those you have influenced by being a change agent.

I believe that Maxine needed the guidance from Nagra. Her angel, Nagra, was in Kenya not making her do anything, but instead she was pushing her toward solid ground. Maxine did not know she needed an anchor, but God did. It's amazing that God knows just when things in our lives are getting a little foggy.

Maxine had some issues going to Africa. She didn't want to go and made up excuses. Anytime you set sail into uncharted waters there will be an initial resistance, a pervading fear, and a fear of the unknown. If you feel this, great: you're human. The enemy will likely try to stop you in your tracks, or tell you you're crazy for trying to find your purpose in the first place. He might say harsh things like: *"You don't deserve to have a purpose,"* or *"You'll never find what you're looking for.*" What you have to know is that this inner dialogue isn't true—it's more afraid than you are. Its main goal is to keep you comfortable.

Maxine like many of us had to combat her inner dialogue. When she stopped paying attention to the thoughts as they were spiraling through her head, they lost their power. They get their evil force by operating below the surface, so when you shine a spotlight of awareness upon them they lose their control over you. But God also helps us with our battles; it would be wise to walk with spiritual discernment, for the Bible says that even the devil will disguise himself as an angel of light. We can always be confident with God's help as He leads us to recognize truth and deception through his Spirit. The Apostle Paul says in **2 Corinthians 11:14**, "*And no marvel; for Satan, himself is transformed into an angel of light.*"

Angels are mighty beings who offer praise and worship to God. God never intends for us to worship angels or pray to them. He alone is worthy of our worship according to **Revelation 4:11**, "*Thou art worthy, O Lord, to receive glory and honour and power: for thou hast created all things, and for thy pleasure they are and were created.*" And angels remind us of this truth. In **Revelation 5:11-12** we read, "*Then I looked and heard the voice of many angels, numbering thousands upon thousands, and ten thousand times ten thousand...In a loud voice they sang: "Worthy is the Lamb, who was slain, to receive power and wealth and wisdom and strength and honor and glory and praise!"*

God promises to help us as we seek to honor Him and walk wisely in this life. We can trust that even when we're unaware of our needs or impending disasters that lay before us, God knows. He is at work—sending words of hope, protecting us, taking care of our needs, and giving us justice when necessary. God also grants us mercy, drawing us closer to Him, and always encouraging us to walk wisely, be aware, and live fully for Him.

God often works in ways we can't fully see, sometimes behind the scenes or with unexpected timing. Yet He's always working on our behalf. Whether we realize it or not, there's a spiritual realm constantly around us. May God give us

eyes to see clearly that angels are among us and that God is working miracles, even today.

Digging Deeper

Don't be afraid to share and discuss your responses, but remember to discuss in love.

In the Greek and Hebrew, the word *angel* refers to a messenger. Messengers can appear as humans but represent God. Messengers may be overwhelmingly awesome, be winged creatures, or be indistinguishable from ordinary people. **1 Chronicles 12:22,** *"For at that time day by day there came to David to help him, until it was a great host, like the host of God."*

When you read this scripture what roles do angels play in God's plan for His world? What roles do they play in our lives?

_____

_____

_____

_____

_____

_____

Luke 1:13, *"But the angel said unto him, Fear not, Zacharias: for thy prayer is heard; and thy wife Elisabeth shall bear thee a son, and thou shalt call his name John."* Have you ever encountered an angel? Do you think you would know it if you did? Do you expect them to look a certain way?

_____

_____

_____

_____

_____

_____

_____

_____

Luke 1:30, "*And the angel said unto her, Fear not, Mary: for thou hast found favour with God.* Would you expect to encounter one?" *The word says in* **Hebrews 13:2,** "*Be not forgetful to entertain strangers: for thereby some have entertained angels unawares.*" *Have you ever missed an opportunity to be blessed by an angel because you doubted they were an angel?*

_____
_____
_____
_____
_____

Once Maxine became familiar with her inner dragons, it was easier to slay them. She needed help from two angels, Nagra and Ms. Lenora Bessemer, to slay her dragons in order to move toward her purpose and destiny? Think about any fears you may have; list them but also think of scriptures you can use to overcome them.

_____
_____
_____
_____
_____

If you had all the money in the world, how would you spend your time? Do you believe that you have a purpose to accomplish something special for the kingdom of God?

_____
_____
_____
_____
_____

What activities set your soul on fire with the spirit and power of the Holy Ghost? Would you do this even if you were not paid for it?

_____

_____

_____

_____

_____

_____

What do you love to do? Are you anointed to do it?

_____

_____

_____

_____

_____

Journal about anything that makes you believe in your heart of hearts that angels have been in your presence.

_____

_____

_____

_____

_____

_____

"An angel working anywhere in the world fulfills God's promise to work all things for the good of all Christians." John Piper

Chapter 6

Rescued Before the Storm

I'm afraid of storms especially if there is a tornado involved. One day, however, magnified that fear. I was out shopping at our local mall. Macy's was having a fantastic pre-sale event, and I was trying to gather a few spring outfits. The young lady behind the register was so kind and we were talking about the pollen count being so high in April. To be exact, it was 5:25 p.m. on April 27, 2011 that my phone starting ringing.

My eyes always have a way of disclosing how I feel about something without me even opening my mouth. So, as I'm looking at my phone my eyes were getting bigger and tears were pooling in the corners. The young lady asked, "Ma'am are you alright?" As I stood there looking not at her but passed her, my mind was traveling back down memory lane. I saw my firstborn, Thaydra, as she was waving good-bye to me on her first day of school at 3 years old. I saw her in my arms at the doctor's office when she had her first seizure of three seizures at 2 years old. I saw her acting crazy and laughing till we cried, while she recited the lines of the movie 'ATL.' I saw her in her prom dress and I remembered leaving her at the University of Alabama eight months before this day on the 14th day of August, 2010.

I vividly remember reading the first of about twenty-five text messages: "A tornado has touched down on the campus of the University of Alabama." "Have you talked to Thaydra?" "A tornado hit her campus." "Some students were killed in a tornado on Thaydra's campus."

I then realized how small, helpless, and powerless I am. My hands began to tremble as I held my phone.

It was hard for me to believe such a devastating tornado had hit Tuscaloosa; the most sports-obsessed city in America (with everyone greeting you with a "Roll Tide"). But on this day, I just wanted the tide to stop rolling and causing all the carnage over my daughter's College town. Throughout the evening, Thaydra's friends, and family were texting, calling, and sending messages on Facebook, trying to determine if she was O.K. Even as the morning sun rose after a rainy night in Georgia, she had no idea her father was heading to Tuscaloosa. It was much later the night before, when Thaydra called to tell us that she and all of the girls of the Parham Dormitory had sat in their basement confused and fear-stricken most of the night. She talked about how they had been praying aloud believing that God would keep them safe. Her father did manage to make it home safely with Thaydra the following day. The events of the day before had changed the way we view storms.

Even Maxine learned that when a storm hits, it can destroy or restore relationships and individual lives. When she was in Kenya, she didn't think about preventing the storm by being honest and telling William everything she knew and had discovered. Sometimes we put ourselves in harm's way. Some storms are out of our control, and others are a direct result of our actions.

We can be mad at God when He allows hard times in our lives, but sometimes the reality is we knew the right answers but chose to go our own way instead. Maxine had information that she was withholding from William; it was her decision to do so. We always have a choice. This is a passage from *Recue Me*: *Maxine's hands dropped to her lap. This was the perfect time to tell him that she had withheld information from him partly out of fear and somewhat out of selfishness. Just say it. But what if Nagra is right, and he doesn't believe me? Am I ready to lose him tonight?*

Maxine opened her mouth to tell him, but stopped at the expression in his eyes. When they settled on hers, dark with emotion, she could almost imagine his next words were going to be a declaration of some kind. I am going to tell him; I just need a little more time. **Instead**, *she said, "When my parents died, I did everything wrong."*

Notice the word *instead*—it signals that she made a decision to do the opposite of what was right. When we are challenged by unknown results we lose our brains and revert to our old ways. The truth is we all face storms in our lives. **Storms.** We all experience them. Storms around us. Storms within us. Sometimes God gives us peace FROM the storm; sometimes He gives us peace IN the storm.

They may not all be as little or insignificant as telling the truth, but we all face them. Sometimes they are thunderstorms that just leave a little bit of damage or ruffled feathers. Sometimes they are tornadoes that wreak havoc and destruction in our lives that take years to rebuild. The question is, what do we do when we are in them? How do we cope? And isn't that just like life; sometimes before we can put one problem to rest, we find ourselves assaulted by another. No one can better testify to that fact than Job.

Job as you may recall faced a series of problems that came one behind another. He hadn't gotten over the trauma and the awesome impact of the first problem before he was hit with another problem. And before he could really come to grips with the first and second problem, he was then assaulted by a third one. And the problems just kept on coming. Sometimes, life is just like that old saying: *"When it rains, it pours."* This is why Job said in **Job 14:1**, *"Man that is born of a woman is of a few days and full of trouble."*

Oftentimes, the warning is given, but because we were not listening, we find ourselves in stormy situations. Simply put, we are launching out too soon when we do something before God says to do it—when we jump into something like a new job, a new relationship without God's endorsement, without God's direction, and without God's blessing. That is moving too soon! In fact, sometimes what we want to do God does not want it for us at all. It may not even be in God's will for our life.

God has given us our own free will, He allows it. I believe sometimes although He has it for us, He doesn't have it for us right now and that is because He knows us better than we know ourselves. God created us and for that reason He knows where our spiritual level is and where it needs to be. God knows if

we have not matured enough in Christ. We may not be ready to survive the storm that is on its way into our lives. Therefore, while it may be true that the LORD has a blessing for us, it may not be right now!

There is somebody reading this study guide right now who is in a storm and it is not a storm that has been around just a little while, but you've been in this storm for a long time. You hoped it would soon pass over, but it is still raging. Some of our lives are getting worse rather than better, in spite of all of our prayers. In spite of all that you've done. The forecast says that another storm is coming in your direction and it may be worse.

Storms can hit your home and cause turbulence for you in your family. Storms can target your church and will cause an entire congregation to fall apart. Storms can affect our health, with one bad report from the doctor. Storms come in many different forms but they all can do damage.

When you do not see any light at the end of your storm, it can make you want to give up. Peter forecast storms but we did not listen to him, for he had warned us before they occurred. In **1 Peter 4:12-13** he said, *"Beloved, think it not strange concerning the fiery trial which is to try you, as though some strange thing happened unto you: But rejoice, inasmuch as ye are partakers of Christ's sufferings; that, when his glory shall be revealed, ye may be glad also with exceeding joy."*

Let me encourage you God needs you to have faith in the storm and say even in the storm, *"I know it's rough and I know it's hard, and the situation is serious but I'm going through! I will come out stronger on the other side."*

Digging Deeper

Don't be afraid to share and discuss your responses, but remember to discuss in love.

Tell your storm story?

_____

_____

_____

_____

_____

_____

As Christians, we need to know that storms happen. **John 16:33,** *"These things I have spoken unto you, that in me ye might have peace. In the world ye shall have tribulation: but be of good cheer; I have overcome the world."* Difficulties, stress, death, and pain—they all happen.

How do we find peace before the storm? Can you endure like a good soldier? Or will you throw down your weapons and give up?

_____

_____

_____

_____

_____

_____

1 Peter 4:12-16 says, *"Beloved, do not be surprised at the fiery trial when it comes upon you to test you, as though something strange were happening to you. But rejoice insofar as you share Christ's sufferings, that you may also rejoice and be glad when his glory is revealed. If you are insulted for the name of Christ, you are blessed, because the Spirit of glory and of God rests upon you. But let none of*

you suffer as a murderer or a thief or an evildoer or as a meddler. Yet if anyone suffers as a Christian, let him not be ashamed, but let him glorify God in that name." God clearly and repeatedly says that we will have trials in our life.

Why do we *"Christians"* question God while facing the storms of life? *Think of a time that you wished your response was different? That you wished you would have taken the time to allow God to speak before you acted.*

_____

_____

_____

_____

_____

_____

Will God always take away the storms in our life? As you consider this question, read Paul's response in **2 Corinthians 12:9-10,** *"But he said to me, 'My grace is sufficient for you, for my power is made perfect in weakness." Therefore, I will boast all the more gladly of my weaknesses, so that the power of Christ may rest upon me. For the sake of Christ, then, I am content with weaknesses, insults, hardships, persecutions, and calamities. For when I am weak, then I am strong."* Now think about a time that God did not move you out of the storm. He allowed the storm to stay and it caused significant damage in your life, your marriage, on your job, in friendships.

Did you still praise God or were you upset? Did you stop going to church? Were you angry with God? Discuss and explain why?

_____

_____

_____

_____

_____

_____

Look at this verse and discuss the struggle Peter had in the storm of **Matthew 14: 30-31,** *"But when he saw the wind, he was afraid, and beginning to sink he cried out, 'Lord, save me.' Jesus immediately reached out his hand and took hold of him, saying to him, 'O you of little faith, why did you doubt?'"* Why do we as Christians doubt God? *If God told you to come would you have gotten out of boat? Would you have said yes to the assignment? Would you have said yes to moving to a new city? Would you have said yes to letting go of a relationship? Be honest and answer below.*

_____
_____
_____
_____
_____
_____
_____
_____

To be honest there are times, when I relate to Peter. In the storm, I begin to focus on the wind and not on my Savior. It's not always but sometimes the storm seems as if it's bigger than God. But those are the times when I have to remember, I don't serve the storm chaser. I serve the storm DESTROYER! *Have you had storms in your life where the wind took your focus off God?*

_____
_____
_____
_____
_____
_____

What types of storms did Jesus face while He was here on the earth?

_____
_____
_____
_____
_____

Daniel 3:1-30, *"King Nebuchadnezzar made an image of gold, whose height was sixty cubits and its breadth six cubits. He set it up on the plain of Dura, in the province of Babylon. 2 Then King Nebuchadnezzar sent to gather the satraps, the prefects, and the governors, the counselors, the treasurers, the justices, the magistrates, and all the officials of the provinces to come to the dedication of the image that King Nebuchadnezzar had set up. 3 Then the satraps, the prefects, and the governors, the counselors, the treasurers, the justices, the magistrates, and all the officials of the provinces gathered for the dedication of the image that King Nebuchadnezzar had set up. And they stood before the image that Nebuchadnezzar had set up. 4 And the herald proclaimed aloud, "You are commanded, O peoples, nations, and languages, 5 that when you hear the sound of the horn, pipe, lyre, trigon, harp, bagpipe, and every kind of music, you are to fall down and worship the golden image that King Nebuchadnezzar has set up. 6 And whoever does not fall down and worship shall immediately be cast into a burning fiery furnace." 7 Therefore, as soon as all the peoples heard the sound of the horn, pipe, lyre, trigon, harp, bagpipe, and every kind of music, all the peoples, nations, and languages fell down and worshiped the golden image that King Nebuchadnezzar had set up. 8 Therefore at that time certain Chaldeans came forward and maliciously accused the Jews. 9 They declared to King Nebuchadnezzar, "O king, live forever! 10 You, O king, have made a decree, that every man who hears the sound of the horn, pipe, lyre, trigon, harp, bagpipe, and every kind of music, shall fall down and worship the golden image. 11 And whoever does not fall down and worship shall be cast into a burning fiery furnace. 12 There are certain Jews whom you have appointed over the affairs of the province of Babylon: Shadrach, Meshach, and Abednego. These men, O king, pay no attention to you; they do not serve your gods or worship the golden image that you have set up." 13 Then Nebuchadnezzar in furious rage commanded that Shadrach, Meshach, and Abednego be brought. So, they brought these men before the king. 14 Nebuchadnezzar answered and said to them, "Is it true, O Shadrach, Meshach, and Abednego, that you do not serve my gods or worship the golden image that I have set up? 15 Now if you are ready when you hear the sound of the horn, pipe, lyre, trigon, harp, bagpipe, and every kind of music, to fall down and worship the image that I have made, well and good. But if you do not worship, you shall immediately be cast into a burning fiery furnace. And who is the god who will deliver you out of my hands?" 16 Shadrach, Meshach, and Abednego answered and said to the king, "O Nebuchadnezzar, we have no need to answer you in this*

matter. 17 If this be so, our God whom we serve is able to deliver us from the burning fiery furnace, and he will deliver us out of your hand, O king. 18 But if not, be it known to you, O king, that we will not serve your gods or worship the golden image that you have set up." 19 Then Nebuchadnezzar was filled with fury, and the expression of his face was changed against Shadrach, Meshach, and Abednego. He ordered the furnace heated seven times more than it was usually heated. 20 And he ordered some of the mighty men of his army to bind Shadrach, Meshach, and Abednego, and to cast them into the burning fiery furnace. 21 Then these men were bound in their cloaks, their tunics, their hats, and their other garments, and they were thrown into the burning fiery furnace. 22 Because the king's order was urgent and the furnace overheated, the flame of the fire killed those men who took up Shadrach, Meshach, and Abednego. 23 And these three men, Shadrach, Meshach, and Abednego, fell bound into the burning fiery furnace. 24 Then King Nebuchadnezzar was astonished and rose up in haste. He declared to his counselors, "Did we not cast three men bound into the fire?" They answered and said to the king, "True, O king." 25 He answered and said, "But I see four men unbound, walking in the midst of the fire, and they are not hurt; and the appearance of the fourth is like a son of the gods." 26 Then Nebuchadnezzar came near to the door of the burning fiery furnace; he declared, "Shadrach, Meshach, and Abednego, servants of the Most High God, come out, and come here!" Then Shadrach, Meshach, and Abednego came out from the fire. 27 And the satraps, the prefects, the governors, and the king's counselors gathered together and saw that the fire had not had any power over the bodies of those men. The hair of their heads was not singed, their cloaks were not harmed, and no smell of fire had come upon them. 28 Nebuchadnezzar answered and said, "Blessed be the God of Shadrach, Meshach, and Abednego, who has sent his angel and delivered his servants, who trusted in him, and set aside the king's command, and yielded up their bodies rather than serve and worship any god except their own God. 29 Therefore I make a decree: Any people, nation, or language that speaks anything against the God of Shadrach, Meshach, and Abednego shall be torn limb from limb, and their houses laid in ruins, for there is no other god who is able to rescue in this way." 30 Then the king promoted Shadrach, Meshach, and Abednego in the province of Babylon."

What type of storm was Shadrach, Meshach, and Abednego facing?

_____

_____

_____

_____

_____

What type of peer pressure do you think they were facing? Have you ever had to deal with peer pressure as a Christian and how did you handle it?

_____

_____

_____

_____

_____

*Look again at **Daniel 3:16-18**. How did they respond to the hardships they faced?*

_____

_____

_____

_____

_____

Did they have a lack of faith because they did not fully believe God would rescue them? Have you ever doubted God would rescue you?

_____

_____

_____

_____

_____

Shadrach, Meshach, and Abednego were in the midst of a storm. They were facing death as a result of not worshipping the idols set up by King Nebuchadnezzar. Look at their response to the king in the scripture again. *"17 If this be so, our God whom we serve is able to deliver us out of your hand, O king. 18 But if not, be it known to you, O king, that we will not serve your gods..."*

Verse 18 proves to be an incredibly powerful verse. They told the king that if God did not deliver them how they thought He should, they still would not serve King Nebuchadnezzar. Shadrach, Meshach, and Abednego were ***T.T.S.P. Christians and B. I. N. Christians, "This too Shall Pass"*** and ***"But If Not"*** Christians. They would not give up. In the midst of trouble and pain, the storm was not going to destroy their testimony or faith in God, even if God did not intervene as they thought God should intervene.

*Do you ever struggle with being a **"But If Not"** and a **"This too Shall Pass"** Christian? If so, how or why?*

_____
_____
_____
_____
_____
_____
_____

Why do you think God would allow his followers to be in storms? Especially if we believe our God is loving.

_____
_____
_____
_____
_____
_____
_____

Have you had a storm in your life that brought you closer to God? Journal about it below.

_____

_____

_____

_____

_____

_____

_____

_____

_____

_____

_____

_____

_____

_____

_____

_____

_____

_____

_____

_____

_____

_____

Chapter 7

Rescued from the Shame of Singleness

Chances are you've never met me but I already know something about you: You are either married or single. You are either singing a duet or a solo. Now I suspect something else about some of you. I suspect that some of you are married but wish you were single. Further, I suspect very strongly that some of you are single but wish you were married. Many of you who are single have a desire to be pursued by a good godly man, and dealing with the overwhelming and painful feelings of not being wanted often results from not having that special someone to love.

But whether you are married or single, you can be happy in the Lord Jesus Christ. I can relate to many of your emotions. In my own season of singleness, I remember those feelings of not feeling wanted. It did something to me each time I watched one of my sisters in Christ walk down the aisle. Don't get me wrong, never once was I unhappy for them, I just wanted to know when would my time arrive. I longed to be loved unconditionally, for someone to treasure me just as I was, with every spot, blemish, and sin. My heart ached for the young man I fell in love with in high school. He was my first love but after a four-year relationship, he found someone else and I wrestled with feelings of rejection. Like many young ladies do today, I felt if I waited it out, he would come to his senses and come back to me. Can I be candid for a moment? I prayed for that young man to come back to me. I even used scriptures to justify that he would, *"Therefore I will look to the Lord; I will wait for the God of my salvation; my God will hear me." Micah 7:7*

Many times, we believe that just because we are good, God must answer our prayers. We know God created the entire universe in only six days. So why does He make us wait sometimes years before He answers our prayers? I had to learn that, it all had to do with God's sovereignty. It was not a matter of if God could have answered that prayer, because God can do anything He desires to do according to **Luke 1:37**, *"For nothing will be impossible with God."* Therefore, I had to understand it was His will and His timing to answer a prayer.

In God's perfect timing, God will answer all our prayers and give us the desires of our heart. I was being so stubborn, that I did not want to understand God had reasons for the doors He opened and closed. **Isaiah 55:8**, makes it plain, *"For my thoughts are not your thoughts, neither are your ways my ways, saith the Lord."* I had to come to the realization that God created me and as the creator, God was in full and complete control of my life and that young man's life. When He has you to wait, you need to trust that He has a good reason for it. If I had rushed the waiting process, I probably would have missed out on what God wanted to do in and through my life during that time. So, what happened next? We moved on with our lives. He has a wonderful family and I do as well.

I'm grateful for the relationship I developed with God during that period of my life. You see I remained single from that day until the day the Lord allowed my husband to see me. What that breakup and heartache did was incredible. God allowed me to be pulled into His love and He smoothed my broken heart through his word. **Jeremiah 29:13** became my war cry, *"And ye shall seek me, and find me, when ye shall search for me with all your heart."* I had to realize just as Maxine did in *Rescue Me*, that *when God is all you have, God is all you need.*

The waiting season is always difficult when you do not allow growth to happen. It is that time when you have to stay focused on the destination and not get tripped up by the journey. *Why do I say this?* Because during the waiting period there will be a lot of distractions. Imagine if you will, being in the waiting room of your doctor's office. You are given a time to arrive but when you get there they are not ready for your arrival.

Now this does not mean the doctor is not going to see you; it just means that there are others ahead of you or you have some documents to sign and fill out. But you stay because you know that today is your scheduled appointment. You don't get upset because you understand that these individuals in the office had a scheduled appointment as well. You don't get distracted by those who come in after you because they, like you have to wait for their appointed time to see the doctor. It's like that in the singleness waiting game. It doesn't matter who gets married before you do, their appointment was scheduled before yours but the God of all relationships has a scheduled appointment time for you.

This is when you really begin to believe **Psalm 84:11** *that God will withhold no good thing from those who walk uprightly*. There is nothing wrong with being single. If we see a beautiful woman or a handsome man who is not married we may think, *"I wonder what is wrong with her, or what is wrong with him?"* When in fact, nothing at all is wrong with that person. But, something might be wrong with them if they were married. It is better to be a single than to marry the wrong person.

Now, I know that you may be upset. Why? Because like so many other singles you are tired of waiting! If you ask any single person and they are honest, they will tell you that they get lonely. All of these things happen because if you are single and not in a relationship you want to get married! Remember the distractions I told you about earlier; someone else's relationship has nothing to do with you.

We love to look at what someone else is doing and question our own lives. But your life has nothing to do with theirs. Let's go back to the doctor's appointment. You may be going in for your yearly physical, but the person ahead of you may be there because he or she has the flu. Now, I know you would love to be in their place in the appointment line, but you better be thankful. I would much rather be seeing the doctor for my yearly physical than to have to be there because I have the flu. This is about you (the individual) and no one else.

There is also something else to remember—all single women are not in their twenties; some are forty, fifty, and older. But there is nothing wrong with them. This is just where they are and some women do not want to be married. One thing I always stress when I am teaching any singles is that they do not know what goes on in someone else's relationship. Therefore, you must focus on your life. I learned this the hard way.

I never thought I would say this in my lifetime, but my mom had a boyfriend after her divorce. It wasn't like the next day; it was years after the fact. Sure, she referred to him as her "friend," but I knew what "friend" meant. My mom had a boyfriend! It was new territory for me and my siblings, and it was terrifying. But we learned it was going to be okay because it was her life, and none of our business. This man was nothing like my dad. No one could be.

To be able to accept those things, I had to navigate my way through a gamut of new emotions, which was scary. But ultimately, a good thing for my mom and her children. This is about moving on, something that is a very different process for everyone. I've come to learn that when a parent feels comfortable and strong enough to date again, that's when you know it's time for you to move on as well. She was ready, and I guess we had to be ready too. So, remember—live YOUR LIFE and not anyone else's.

I love the prayer that Maxine prayed in *Rescue Me*. William looked at her, and she kept her eyes pinned on the door that had just closed. Maxine was left with William, two pilots, and a stewardess. She felt the heat rise in her cheeks. She remembered that night of their kiss all too well, but there was nothing to worry about because William turned to pick up his folders and went into the other room.

Maxine knew this was going to be a tremendous test of her faith walk so she prayed, *"Lord, I understand that being single is a time for me to reflect upon what it is that makes me happy, what I can do to improve myself. Right now, I need You as I spend this time with William, because deep down inside I know that I am learning more about myself since meeting him. But Father, You are teaching me how to love me just as I am, loving the person I see naked in the mirror, and loving*

You because You have always loved me just as I am. So, on this journey to Kenya, let it be an opportunity for me to do what makes me happy, let it be an opportunity to think about my future and bring me closer to You God by helping those who cannot help themselves, even William. Amen

I wanted to stress in the novel that Maxine had to realize that she was important, beautiful, and whole whether she was in a relationship with William or not. Maxine asked God to allow her to help others during her season of waiting. Maxine's singleness was her assigned portion from God. It was God's gift to her. Your singleness ought not to be viewed as a problem to you but instead it should be viewed as an opportunity for a promotion in God.

A promotion from God? A gift? Yes! Paul says in **1 Corinthians 7:7**, *"Sometimes I wish everyone were single like me—a simpler life in many ways! But celibacy is not for everyone any more than marriage is. God gives the gift of the single life to some, the gift of the married life to others."*

As a single person, you have the opportunity to freely serve in ways that may not be possible with a family. These are the freedoms that allow you to plan your life in ways that many married couples cannot. If you desire, you can travel the world on mission trips; this may be the prime time to develop relationships with your peers that could last a lifetime. Do you play tennis, golf, or any other sport? Guess what? Your singleness allows you to do this without having to worry about being home to cook for your husband or dropping the kids off at their soccer practice. You can go on retreats for your spiritual growth or just read and study the Word of God.

The one thing I know for sure is that you must trust the plan of God for your life. **Jeremiah 29:11,** *"For I know the thoughts that I think toward you, saith the LORD, thoughts of peace, and not of evil, to give you an expected end."* Trust that no matter where you are, if God plans for you to marry, He will lead you to just the right person, and at the right time. Don't believe the lie that the world tells you. "Girl, if you want a man you better get out and find him because he won't be at church." That's a lie from the pits of hell. First, God does not want you as

the woman to find a husband. **Proverbs 18:22,** *"Whoso findeth a wife findeth a good thing, and obtaineth favour of the Lord."*

I love that scripture because God is precise when He says, *findeth a wife.* Do not get tricked into thinking that you have to go with your girls to the clubs to find a man. When God gets ready for you to meet your mate, He will position you for that meeting. It could be in that same doctor's office we discussed earlier, it could be at a gas station, grocery store, skating rink, football game, or God be praised—at the church!

Can I say this to my single sisters? Do not be ashamed because you are waiting! Maintaining your standards are important! Many women have been tricked into not keeping their standards because they met someone who convinced them to let what they believed to be cast into the sea and forgotten. Wouldn't you rather wait than to settle for someone who does not meet the standards that God set for you? Standards are what sets you apart from other women. Your standard is really your dating insurance plan and the premium is paid every time you are saved from getting involved with the wrong person or saying yes to a mess. Keep your standards because they are there to protect you.

Do not listen to the noise around you that tells you to lower your standards. In other words, they are telling you to change who you are and what you believe. But the Word of God says in **Ephesians 3:20,** *"Now unto him that is able to do exceeding abundantly above all that we ask or think, according to the power that worketh in us."* God knows what you desire and because He loves you, He will give you the desires of your heart. Do not get restless in your wait. Because while you wait remember no one can love you better than God.

God's love does not come with the stipulation that sex must be part of the deal. No, true love will wait for God's plan to be in place. Our joy, our complete fulfillment can be found in God and not in a onetime sexual opportunity that leaves you filled with the guilt of sin. This is important for all of us to remember romance is not based on sex. Living a life that is pure is not wrong. It does not matter what everyone else is doing. Do not fall for the devil's Okie Dok.

In *Rescue Me*, the devil challenged God about Maxine's love for him. Let's look back at this passage, '*The devil had boldly laughed, "Lord, I do understand why You love this young woman. She's everything a Father would want in a daughter. Do You truly believe that Maxine Barker will still be as dedicated to You if she finds something or someone to love more than You? I have seen many Christian women give up their commitment for You and walk away for money, sex, and power. They are even trapped by the temptation for the love of not a good man but one of my many counterfeit men." The devil stressed to God that Maxine was no different from every other woman and he was certain she would fail.*'

The devil wants you to believe that you can't wait, but I like your odds with God! God was the one who created you and He said you were good and very good. You are His child. It is also impossible for you to care about you more than God does! So, moments of temptation will come, but moments will always go. Remain strong and faithful because faithless is a bad investment. Don't get caught up because the fall is a long way down. You want the package deal that comes with always and forever. Why? Because you are worth the wait. Don't worry, the one that God has hand picked out for you will meet the standards God set for you!

The next time someone ask you when are you getting married? Tell them when my standards have been met.

Singleness is not a problem; it's a promised gift from God. As long as God is with you, you will never be alone.

Digging Deeper

Don't be afraid to share and discuss your responses, but remember to discuss in love.

Do you have the right attitude about the "gift" of singleness? If so, explain and discuss.

_____

_____

_____

_____

_____

As a single person, do you ever feel that something's wrong with you? If so, how do you deal with that feeling—is it the sort of thing you ignore, or the sort of thing you talk about with someone else to see if it's true?

_____

_____

_____

_____

_____

How might emotional scars from your past actually be telling a different story about why you are single?

_____

_____

_____

_____

_____

How often do you feel really lonely? What sort of relationships do you cultivate in your life to keep from getting lonely?

_____
_____
_____
_____
_____
_____
_____
_____
_____
_____

How do you deal with sadness and jealousy when a friend gets engaged or married, announces she's pregnant, or talks about her sex life?

_____
_____
_____
_____
_____

What do healthy "boundaries" look like as a single person?

_____
_____
_____
_____

Can single women and single men of comparable dating ages "just be friends," and if so, how?

_____
_____
_____
_____

Is it wrong for you to take the initiative with a man and to pursue a potential romantic relationship with him? If you go out of our way to try to meet a husband, does that mean you are not trusting God's sovereignty?

_____
_____
_____
_____
_____
_____
_____
_____
_____
_____
_____
_____

Explain how you use standards in your life to measure your worth.

_____
_____
_____
_____
_____
_____
_____
_____
_____
_____
_____

What does it look like to date Christianly as an older single?

_____
_____
_____
_____
_____

As a single woman committed to following Jesus, how can my commitment to sexual purity be spiritually productive among my non-Christian friends who consider this utterly bizarre?

_____

_____

_____

_____

_____

When you're in ministry with a married man, do you go out of your way to include his wife when you communicate with him on emails, texts, and so on?

_____

_____

_____

_____

_____

How do you fit into your church family, when you feel invisible every Sunday as an older single person without children (or as a divorced or widowed woman)?

_____

_____

_____

_____

_____

How would you address the challenges of single mothers and how to make them feel welcome in social settings?

_____

_____

_____

_____

_____

With regard to contemporary dating practices, what's off-limits for Christians?

_____

_____

_____

_____

_____

Journal about your life as a single Christian. Has it encouraged you or frustrated you to the point that you want to give up believing that God has a mate for you?

_____

_____

_____

_____

_____

_____

_____

_____

_____

_____

_____

_____

_____

_____

_____

_____

_____

_____

_____

Works Cited

Nih.Gov, Substance Abuse and Mental Health Services Administration (US), 2014, www.ncbi.nlm.nih.gov/books/NBK207197/. Accessed 17 May 2019.

Psych Central. (2018, October 8). Understanding the Effects of Trauma: Post-traumatic Stress Disorder (PTSD). Retrieved April 13, 2019, from Psych Central website: https://psychcentral.com/lib/understanding-the-effects-of-trauma-post-traumatic-stress-disorder.

Schrijvers, D.L., De Bruijn, E.R.A., Destoop, M., Hulstijn, W. and Sabbe, B.G.C. (2010). The impact of perfectionism and anxiety traits on action monitoring in major depressive disorder. *Journal of Neural Transmission*, [online] 117(7), pp.869–880